ALIEN PET GOES BERSERK!

When the Veeblax first lunged out of my arms and attached itself to Misty, I thought it was just playing. And when Misty started to scream, I thought she was just being Misty. But when she tried to pull the Veeblax off her chest and I saw it clinging to her in a desperate way, I realized that something stranger was going on.

I jumped to my feet and grabbed the little creature. "Come on, Veeb," I said, tugging at it. "Let go of her!"

The Veeblax only shrieked and clung to Misty even more tightly.

I pulled harder. The Veeblax began to stretch. The combination of its squeals and Misty's screams was starting to make my *sphen-gnut-ksher* throb.

I pulled still harder.

Misty backed away from me.

The Veeblax stretched in my hands until I began to fear it would snap.

"Wow!" yelled someone. "Just like hot mozzarella!"

ALSO IN THIS BOOK:
The stunning final chapter of
"DISASTER ON GEEMBOL SEVEN"

Books by Bruce Coville

The A.I. Gang Trilogy
   Operation Sherlock
   Robot Trouble
   Forever Begins Tomorrow

Bruce Coville's Alien Adventures
   Aliens Ate My Homework
   I Left My Sneakers in Dimension X
   The Search for Snout
   Aliens Stole My Body

Camp Haunted Hills
   How I Survived My Summer Vacation
   Some of My Best Friends Are Monsters
   The Dinosaur That Followed Me Home

I Was a Sixth Grade Alien
   I Was a Sixth Grade Alien
   The Attack of the Two-Inch Teacher
   I Lost My Grandfather's Brain
   Peanut Butter Lover Boy
   Zombies of the Science Fair
   Don't Fry My Veeblax!

Magic Shop Books
   Jennifer Murdley's Toad
   Jeremy Thatcher, Dragon Hatcher
   The Monster's Ring
   The Skull of Truth

My Teacher Books
   My Teacher Is an Alien
   My Teacher Fried My Brains
   My Teacher Glows in the Dark
   My Teacher Flunked the Planet

BRUCE COVILLE

DON'T FRY
MY VEEBLAX!

Illustrated by Tony Sansevero

A
MINSTREL®
BOOK

Published by POCKET BOOKS
New York   London   Toronto   Sydney   Singapore

A MINSTREL PAPERBACK *Original*

 A Minstrel Book published by
POCKET BOOKS, a division of Simon & Schuster Inc.
1230 Avenue of the Americas, New York, NY 10020

 © 1999 Fox Family Properties, Inc.
Fox Family and the Family Channel name and logo are the
respective trademarks of Fox and I.F.E., Inc. All Rights Reserved.

Text copyright © 2000 by Bruce Coville
Illustrations copyright © 2000 by Tony Sansevero

ISBN: 0-671-02655-0

First Minstrel Books printing May 2000

10 9 8 7 6 5 4 3 2 1

A MINSTREL BOOK and colophon are registered trademarks of
Simon & Schuster Inc.

YTV is a registered trademark of YTV Canada, Inc.
© 1999 YTV Canada, Inc.
A Corus™ Entertainment Company

Cover art by Miro Sinovcic

Printed in the U.S.A.

For Gary Delfiner
Friend, Believer, Macher

CHAPTER
1
[TIM]

The Flying Hamster

The whole mess with Pleskit's Veeblax got started because of Percy the Mad Poet.

Pleskit, of course, is the son of the ambassador from the planet Hevi-Hevi, and the first alien kid to go to school on Earth. Or maybe not; though Pleskit is the first alien kid that everyone knows about, from what he tells me there may have been others here in secret. Anyway, he's the only purple kid *I* ever met, and the only kid in our school who comes to class with a bodyguard.

He's also my best friend.

And Percy? His full name is Percy Mortimer Canterfield, and he's this poet who comes to our school every year to do a writing workshop with us. Why the school has to bring in someone special to teach us about writing I'm not sure, since our teachers have us write all year anyway. But Percy has published a couple of books, and as far as I can tell all he ever thinks about is writing, so I suppose he has some useful tips. Besides, he's pretty cool. So I don't mind when he visits. In fact, I kind of like it. He makes poetry more interesting than you would have thought possible.

When Jordan Lynch got put in our class two years ago and heard a poet named Percy was coming to teach us writing for a week, the first words out of his mouth were, "Great. Five days with some skinny sissy spouting off about flowers and bunnies and crap like that."

So it was pretty amusing to see Jordan's face when Percy actually showed up. *Sissy* is not a word you could safely use about this guy. He's tall, about six feet, and definitely looks like he works out on a regular basis. He reminds me a little of Captain Lance Driscoll from *Tarbox Moon Warriors*, except that his nose is slightly bent from where it was broken in a fight.

Linnsy Vanderhof, my upstairs neighbor and former best friend (until she outgrew me), says she likes Percy's broken nose because it keeps him from being a pretty boy. This brings up the only thing I don't like about having Percy visit, namely that some of the girls get all goopy over him—including Linnsy, who really ought to know better.

Anyway, when Percy came this year, he decided we should write poems about pets—which meant that first we had to have a discussion about our pets. I sighed. Pets are a topic I personally find quite distressing, mostly because I don't have one.

"That's all right," said Percy when I pointed this out to him. "You can write about one of the class pets instead."

He was referring to our hamsters. We have three of the little beasts: Ronald Roundbutt, Doris the Delightful, and Hubert Hugecheeks. Hubert got his name the day we all watched in horrified fascination as he crammed so much food into his cheeks that we thought his head might explode.

You should have seen him! Anyway, I like the hamsters, but I don't have what you would call a close personal relationship with any of them.

"I bet I've got the most unusual pet in the class," said Larrabe Hicks proudly.

I doubted this was true; it was far more likely that Pleskit's pet Veeblax was more unusual, since it was the only one on the planet. Even so, I was interested to hear what Larrabe had.

So was Percy. "Why don't you tell us about it?" he said.

Larrabe beamed. "I have a woodchuck. His name is Harold."

"A woodchuck?" cried Jordan. "That's the craziest thing I ever heard!" He would have said more, but he got laughing so hard that Brad Kent—who could be Jordan's personal pet, since he seems to look at Jordan the way most dogs look at their masters—had to pound him on the back to stop him from choking.

"Sounds pretty cool to me," said Percy. "Any chance you could bring him in?"

This was a typical Percy thing to do. He was always suggesting something that made our teachers groan and roll their eyes. Only Ms.

Weintraub didn't, because she is very cool, definitely the coolest teacher we've ever had. She actually agreed that if it was okay with Larrabe's mother, Harold could spend the week with us.

The next morning I got to school a little early, something that doesn't happen all that often. Pleskit and I were talking about plans for the weekend (even though it was only Tuesday). His bodyguard, McNally, who is sort of my hero, was standing a few feet away.

(My mother doesn't like me to call adults by their last names, since she thinks it's rude, but that's what McNally prefers. "The name's McNally—just McNally" is the way he introduces himself. This has led Shhh-foop, the embassy cook, to believe that his proper name is "Just McNally.")

As Pleskit and I talked, McNally's eyes were roving the classroom, checking everything out. At least, that's my theory. I have no idea what his eyes were really doing, since I've never seen them. McNally always wears dark sunglasses, even inside.

5

Suddenly he began to smile. "Well, I'll be danged," he muttered.

I turned toward where he was looking.

Larrabe had just come through the door. He was holding a leash. At the other end of the leash, strapped into a leather harness, was a woodchuck!

Larrabe's mom walked in behind him, carrying a big metal cage.

"Told you I had a woodchuck," said Larrabe happily. He reached down and lifted the creature onto his desk. "Meet Harold!"

Harold turned out to be pretty cute, in an oversized, rodenty sort of way. He was almost two feet long, with short legs, thick fur, big black eyes, and a lot of blubber. ("Harold *loves* to eat," explained Larrabe. "It's one of his favorite things in life.")

Harold was amazingly tame for something you usually consider to be a wild animal and he sat on Larrabe's desk without moving, even while the whole class clustered around to get a good look at him.

"I thought that kind of critter was called a groundhog," said Chris Mellblom.

"Woodchucks and groundhogs are just different names for the same animal," said Larrabe, rummaging in his backpack.

"How much ground would a groundhog hog if a groundhog could hog ground?" muttered Jordan.

"They're also called whistle-pigs in some places," added Larrabe, continuing to rummage in his pack and ignoring Jordan's comment. "Ah, here we go."

He pulled a carrot out of his pack and held it over Harold's head. Immediately the woodchuck lurched onto his hindquarters and began reaching for it.

"Ooooh, that's so-o-o-o cute!" cried about eight girls in unison.

Given how mellow the woodchuck was, who would have figured it would be such a disaster when he met Hubert Hugecheeks? Actually, the problem was mostly on Hubert's side, since he was the one who seemed to have a psychological meltdown when Misty Longacres brought him over to meet Harold.

Now this was a typical dippy Misty idea. I mean, a girl who has three cats ought to know that just because something looks sweet and cuddly doesn't mean it won't have a vicious streak.

On the other hand, it's not like hamsters are normally cold-blooded killers or anything.

Anyway, Misty—who was probably getting annoyed because Harold was getting more attention than she was—came running over to Larrabe's desk with Hubert cupped in her hands and said, "Look, Hubie, here's a big brother for you!" Dumping him on the desk, she said, "Aren't they cute together?"

Hubert did not seem to think so. In fact, when Misty put him on the desk, he totally wigged out.

It was the first time I had ever seen a hamster hiss.

Harold reared back on his hind legs and made a shrill whistling sound.

People began to shout. Misty, realizing she had made a big mistake, reached down to grab Hubert.

Hubert, still gripped by his psychotic breakdown, sank his teeth into Misty's fingertip.

He must have bit in pretty deep, because when Misty screamed and yanked her hand into the air, Hubert came with it.

He made it to about shoulder level before his teeth unhooked.

All the girls began to scream—well, I let out a little yelp, too—as Hubert hurtled toward the front wall of the classroom and what looked to be a truly ugly death.

CHAPTER
2
[L I N N S Y]

Percy the Mad Poet

When I saw Hubert go flying through the air, I let out a little scream. When I remembered this later I was a little annoyed at myself, because I don't want to be the kind of girl who makes those little screamy noises. But really, the sight of that poor hamster heading for a collision that would splatter his guts across the wall just dragged the sound out of me.

Then I saw that Percy the Mad Poet had climbed onto Ms. Weintraub's chair. He had on Jordan's baseball glove, which he had confiscated the day before because Jordan kept putting it on Tim's head. Thrusting his hand into the air, Percy snatched the hurtling Hubert in mid-flight, swinging his arm down gracefully so that he was cradling the hamster in front of him.

We all applauded. Well, all of us except Misty, who suddenly started to scream, "Rabies! I'm gonna get rabies!"

Ms. Weintraub put an arm around her shoulder and said firmly, "Let's go to the nurse, dear. And no, you are *not* going to get rabies."

The rest of us, who were used to this kind of thing from Misty, continued applauding.

"Thank you," said Percy, stepping down from the chair and taking a bow. "Thank you very much."

Holding out the glove, he walked around showing us Hubert so that we could see he was all right. The little guy sat there, blinking and looking a little groggy, but otherwise none the worse for his adventure.

Is it any wonder we girls all thought Percy was so . . . well, *wonderful?* Plus, I wish you could hear the way that man could use words! "The night sky's velvet curtain" and "Captured by spring's wild rapture" and "The cold caress of death's icy fingers." All I can say is, I wish the boys in our class could talk half that well every once in a while.

After Ms. Weintraub got back from taking Misty to the nurse, she called the class to order, which wasn't easy under the circumstances. "Misty is fine," she said. "There was a lot more blood than there was cut."

"Is she gonna get rabies?" asked Rafaella Cruz.

Ms. Weintraub sighed. "No, she is *not* going to get rabies. Think for a second, Rafaella. If

Misty could get rabies from Hubert, then all of us would all have been in danger of that every day. It's simply not a problem with domestic pets that are kept indoors, or properly vaccinated."

"What about Harold?" asked Michael Wu. "Woodchucks aren't domestic. At least, not normally."

"We got him when he was just a pup," said Larrabe, putting a protective arm around Harold. "That's what they call baby woodchucks, pups. And he's had his shots, just like a dog or cat. He's plenty safe. Besides, he's not the one who bit Misty. It was that vicious hamster."

"Now listen," said Ms. Weintraub. "After what we've just seen, I'm certain you all realize that you have to be careful when putting animals that aren't used to one another in the same place. Even so, I have a suggestion that I think will be fun. Why don't we organize a pet show to go along with the collection of poetry Mr. Canterfield is helping us put together? We could do it in the gym—that would give us plenty of room to keep the pets apart. I think it would be a fun way to celebrate publishing our anthology!"

Everyone thought this was a wonderful idea. Well, almost everyone; Jordan, of course, thought it "sucked"—though he didn't say that too loudly.

"I wonder if the Fatherly One will allow me to bring my Veeblax," said Pleskit.

"What's a Veeblax?" asked Larrabe.

"My pet shapeshifter," said Pleskit.

"Yeah, right," snorted Jordan.

"Pleskit's serious," said Tim.

"A serious nutcase," sneered Jordan.

"I've seen the Veeblax!" said Tim hotly. "It's totally cool. It can turn itself into all kinds of things. I even taught it to do the Frankenstein walk."

"Can it imitate a nerd?" asked Jordan.

This burst of wit sent Brad Kent into gales of laughter.

"Look, Pleskit," continued Jordan. "You can say you've got anything you want in that flying saucer where you live, and how would we know if it's true or not? The only person you ever let into the place is nerdbutt here." (By "nerdbutt" he meant Tim, of course.) "I'll believe you've got a pet that can change shape when I see it with my own eyes."

Pleskit didn't say anything. But he got a stubborn look on his face, and I had a feeling he was going to do everything he could to bring the Veeblax to school, pet show or no pet show.

CHAPTER
3
[PLESKIT]

Wakkam Akkim

When McNally and I got back to the embassy that afternoon, I found most of the staff gathered around the kitchen table.

"Where is the Fatherly One?" I asked, dumping my bookbag beside the door and climbing into my chair. "I want to talk to him about taking the Veeblax to school."

"He's rather distracted right now," said Beezle Whompis.

Beezle Whompis is the Fatherly One's secretary. He only comes to the kitchen for companionship, since he is an energy being and does not eat regular food.

"Distracted?" I asked nervously. "Is there some new problem?"

"No problem," said Beezle Whompis, flickering briefly out of sight. (It's difficult for him to maintain a physical form, and he only does it to make it easier for the rest of us to talk to him.) "Just an important visitor expected."

"An off-worlder?" I asked excitedly.

"His new *wakkam*," said Ms. Buttsman, our protocol officer, and the only Earthling on the staff besides McNally. "Whatever that is."

"A *wakkam* is what you Earthlings might call a 'guru,' " put in Barvgis, the Fatherly One's slimeball assistant. (I don't mean *slimeball* in the negative way that Earthlings use the word. I just mean that Barvgis is nearly round and quite slimy. But he's also a very pleasant being.) He belched contentedly, then added, "Actually, the more precise translation would probably be 'spiritual massagemaster.' "

"Care for a snack, my little Pleskit-pie?" crooned Shhh-foop, sliding over to the table and twirling her orange tentacles in excitement. "I have some *pak-skwardles* made just fresh for you."

"I'd love some!" I said.

"And some coffee for the handsome Just McNally?" sang Shhh-foop.

"Uh, sure, why not," said McNally. He sighed as Shhh-foop slid happily back to the counter. Though she offers coffee to McNally on a daily basis, our Queen of the Kitchen has not yet mastered the art of making this Earthly beverage.

Barvgis picked a squirmer out of the bowl in front of him. Ignoring its tiny screams, he bit off its head. Then he turned to me. Using full Hevi-Hevian speech, he said, "The *wakkam*'s complete and proper name is *Wakkam* Akkim <fruity smell> Elba [small fart of acceptance] Bonga. She is considered a great adviser, and it is an honor for your Fatherly One to be accepted as her student."

I was anxious to meet the *wakkam* myself, since I knew she would be a very important person in the Fatherly One's life. Besides, it was quite possible she would be my own *wakkam* when I reached the age of *vershniffle*. It also occurred to me that I might get some advice from her about dealing with Jordan, or at least the feelings Jordan so easily provokes in me.

"Just why is this, uh, *wakkam* considered a great adviser?" asked Ms. Buttsman.

"*Wakkam* Akkim trained with a long line of *wakkams*," said Barvgis, pulling the tail of a squirmer from between his teeth.

Ms. Buttsman turned her head, looking as if she had just smelled something bad. But then, she almost always looks that way. I do not think the world meets with Ms. Buttsman's approval.

Barvgis continued as if he had not noticed. "*Wakkam* Akkim's immediate trainer was *Wakkam* Garboola, who was the greatest peacemaker of his time. *Wakkam* Akkim herself gained prominence when—"

Barvgis stopped, looking uncomfortable. The Fatherly One had just entered the room. This was relatively unusual; he did not often sit in the kitchen with us.

"A snack for the high and lordly Meenom?" sang Shhh-foop, sliding eagerly to the table.

"Not now, thank you, Shhh-foop," said the Fatherly One. "Go on, all of you—don't let me interrupt you. I just thought I would wait here until the *wakkam* arrived."

Despite his attempts to appear casual, I noticed the Fatherly One was making small farts of nervousness, which is unusual for him.

It did not seem to be a good time to approach him about taking the Veeblax to school. Even so, I was getting up my nerve to discuss the idea when the speaker above the door belched for our attention, then said, "Transport pod approaching! Docking time will be three minutes and twenty-two seconds."

"*Zgribnick!*" cried the Fatherly One. "The *wakkam* is almost here." He glanced around the table. "Do I look all right?"

Ms. Buttsman reached out and straightened his collar, a gesture I thought was highly inappropriate.

"You look fine, sir," she said, in a nicer tone of voice than she has ever used with me.

"All right, everyone," said the Fatherly One. "Let us greet our visitor."

Wakkam Akkim entered the embassy via a transport tube. She smiled when she saw us all standing there. "Greetings!" she chirped. "I wish you love and understanding."

She walked to the Fatherly One. "Meenom Ventrah?" she asked, putting out a three-fingered hand.

"Your new *plissinga*," responded the Fatherly One, bowing his head in respect.

The *wakkam* was fairly short, only about a head taller than me. She had a beakish nose and tufts of blue feathers for eyebrows and hair. Her three-fingered hands were scaly and ended in sharp claws. Her skin was yellow, her eyes round and dark black. She wore a feathered robe, and a cape that was kept from the floor by tiny flying creatures.

That was all interesting. But what I liked best was the humble, loving quality that seemed to radiate from her. I quickly felt comfortable in her presence.

Unfortunately, she and the Fatherly One soon disappeared for a conference, and I realized I had not yet discussed with him the question of bringing the Veeblax to school.

The Fatherly One is very busy, and when he still had not become available by the next morning, I made an executive decision of my own: I would take the Veeblax to school, in order to show Jordan that I had indeed been telling the truth.

This was not entirely wise. It would have been better to wait and get the Fatherly One's permission. But I did not want to listen to Jordan sneering and jeering about the fact that I had failed to produce the Veeblax.

I recognize this as a failing on my part. I should know better than to respond to teasing and sarcasm. But it is not always easy to remain calm in the face of such obnoxiousness. So I packed a large container of Veeblax chow, which is purple and quite fragrant. Then I put my beloved pet into its carrying case and headed for the limo.

McNally shook his head when he saw me. "Pleskit, are you sure you want to do this?" he asked.

"Is there any reason I should not?"

"Maybe you should ask that question of your Fatherly One."

"He is not available," I said, more sharply than I meant to. I looked at McNally. "Are you going to stop me?"

He shrugged. "I'm going to strongly advise

23

you not to. But I can't stop you. That's not part of my job description. I'm just here to protect you from harm. If you want to shoot yourself in the foot, that's your own problem."

I have noticed that Earthlings tend to use very violent metaphors.

Unfortunately, as it turned out, the only problem with this metaphor was that it wasn't strong enough.

Shooting myself in the foot would probably have been pleasant compared to the events that followed.

CHAPTER
4
[TIM]

Misty and the Veeblax

I was really bummed about the pet show idea, mostly because it rubbed my face in one of the most rotten facts about my life, namely, that my mother won't let me have a dog, or a cat, or even a hamster, for Pete's sake!

"I know you too well, Tim," she says, whenever I ask for one. "You'll be all enthusiastic at first, but sooner or later *I'm* going to end up taking care of it. And I just don't have time for that."

If my father was still around, I bet *he'd* let me have a dog. But I can't think about that too much, because if I do I start to get a little crazy. So mostly I just bug Mom about it.

The fact that we live in an apartment build-ing in the city makes it harder to convince her, since we can't just open the door to let King (that's the name I have for the dog I don't have) out to do his business. Someone would have to walk him. And it doesn't make any difference how often I tell Mom that I would gladly do it, she doesn't trust me to live up to my promise.

What really stinks is that if I think about it too much, I think she might be right.

But that doesn't explain why we can't have a cat, or a hamster, or something. Cripe, I'd even settle for a guinea pig. But Mom claims she had one herself when she was a kid and it was a dis-aster. "It was pretty cute," she told me, "but once it connected the sound of the refrigerator door with getting fed, it shrieked so loud when-ever anyone opened the fridge that the entire family ended up hating the poor thing."

I tried to ask Grampa Zislowski about this, but he just shook his head and muttered, "Guinea pig! Feh. Stupidest thing I ever let that girl talk me into."

So I guess maybe it's true.

Anyway, what was also true was that I did

not have a pet to write about, much less to bring to the pet show—a fact that I felt even more intensely when Pleskit showed up with the Veeblax the next day.

I glanced at McNally. He didn't look entirely happy about this.

The kids, however, were ecstatic. They went crazy over the little guy.

I could understand that. Not only is the Veeblax cute, he is also cool, fascinating, and (occasionally) very scary.

"I think he must be a metaphor for something," said Percy in astonishment after he had watched the Veeblax turn itself into a perfect imitation of my face. "Only I'm not sure what!"

It was easy to see he was thinking about creating a new poetry assignment based on the Veeblax's shapeshifting.

I was proud that I already knew the Veeblax, and could even get him to do some of his best tricks. (You should have seen him imitating Larrabe's woodchuck; you couldn't tell one from the other!)

Pleskit had some Veeblax chow along with him. When he opened the container, the smell that drifted out was so appealing I was almost tempted to try some myself. Larrabe's wood-chuck—which was in its cage in the corner—sat up and began sniffing excitedly.

"Can Harold have some of that?" asked Larrabe.

Pleskit paused. "I don't think so," he said at last. "There's no telling what effect it might have on an Earth animal."

Larrabe sighed and went to give Harold a carrot.

Pleskit pulled a furry nugget of Veeblax chow out of the container. Holding it up, he demonstrated how the Veeblax would imitate a shape in order to get it.

Naturally, after that, *everyone* wanted to feed the critter. That wasn't possible, of course; the Veeblax probably would have exploded if it ate something from everyone. Even so, people managed to get the critter to look like a pile of textbooks, a lunchbox, and a miniature Ms. Weintraub, which got most of us really hysterical.

One of the things everyone thought was interesting was how the Veeblax could change not only its shape but its size.

"Only within certain limits," explained Pleskit, when Michael asked about it. "It has these little air sacs all over its body, sort of like thousands of tiny balloons. By sucking air into the sacs, it can make itself bigger. That's part of how it changes its shape, too." He looked down at the Veeblax. "We have to stop feeding it now, or it's going to get a bellyache."

"That's not fair!" whined Misty. "I didn't get my turn yet."

"What makes you think it would have done anything for you anyway, Misty?" asked Jordan.

I was a little surprised by this, since Jordan usually reserves most of his nasty cracks for me. Then I remembered that he had been going out with Misty's big sister, and they had broken up a little while ago.

Misty glared at him.

Jordan just smirked.

"All right, everyone," said Ms. Weintraub. "Head for your seats. We've got a lot to do today. Mr. Canterfield, do you want to start your lesson?"

Percy went to the front of the room and started giving us some tips for making the images in our poems more clear and strong. After he left we did some other work. Then it was time for lunch, and recess. It was fairly chilly outside—a typical November day in Syracuse—but Pleskit took the Veeblax out anyway.

"It likes cool air," he explained.

We were on the playground, messing around with the Veeblax with a whole crowd of kids around us, when Misty Longacres elbowed her way through the group. "I bet I can get it to come to me," she said smugly, bending over and reaching for the Veeblax.

With a squeal of delight, it leaped up and attached itself to her chest.

Misty squealed, too, but not in delight. "Get it off!" she screamed, staggering back and try-ing to pull the Veeblax away from her. *"GET IT OFF!"*

Shrieking in outrage, the Veeblax only clung to her more tightly.

CHAPTER
5
[PLESKIT]

Fatal Attraction

When the Veeblax first lunged out of my arms and attached itself to Misty, I thought it was just playing. And when Misty started to scream, I thought she was just being Misty. But when she tried to pull the Veeblax off her chest and I saw it clinging to her in a desperate way, I realized that something stranger was going on.

I jumped to my feet and grabbed the little creature. "Come on, Veeb," I said, tugging at it. "Let go of her!"

The Veeblax only shrieked and clung to Misty even more tightly.

I pulled harder.

The Veeblax began to stretch.

The combination of its squeals and Misty's screams was starting to make my *sphen-gnut-ksher* throb.

I pulled still harder.

Misty backed away from me.

The Veeblax stretched in my hands until I began to fear it would snap.

"Wow!" yelled someone. "Just like hot mozzarella!"

McNally came running over. "Pleskit!" he bellowed. "What the heck is going on here?"

"I am not sure!" I answered, shouting myself to be heard above Misty's screams. "I think the Veeblax has fallen in love or something."

This caused Misty to shriek even louder. If she had been from Hevi-Hevi, I'm sure she would have fallen into *kleptra*. I was in danger of doing so myself.

"Get it off!" she screamed, slapping at the Veeblax, which was also shrieking. "Get it off!"

"Don't hit it!" I yelled. "That won't do any good!"

Other kids had gathered in a circle around us. Some were laughing, others screaming.

"Pleskit!" cried Ms. Weintraub, who had come running over close behind McNally. "Do something!"

In desperation I realized there was only one way to get the Veeblax to release its grip on Misty. Closing my eyes, I took a deep breath. Then I gave it a blast of energy from my *sphen-gnut-ksher,* much as I had done to Jordan my first day of school.

With a shriek the Veeblax released its grip on Misty. Its stretched-out body parts retracted so rapidly you could hear them snap.

Misty didn't move at all. She just stood where she was, screaming and crying.

I, of course, fell to the ground in a momentary state of stupefaction as a result of the energy I had just expended. The Veeblax lay beside me, whimpering and panting. I pulled it close, my insides twisting with guilt. Though I felt bad about zapping the Veeblax, that was not the main source of my guilt. I knew that I had not really hurt it, and using my *sphen-gnut-ksher* had at least ended the horrifying episode.

What I felt guilty about was that I had brought the Veeblax to school at all.

McNally knelt beside me, talking quietly while Ms. Weintraub herded the class back inside.

"I think this is another bad one, buddy," he said, massaging my hands.

I blinked. "Misty is not hurt, is she?"

"Nah, she's fine. It's not her injuries I'm worried about. It's her mouth. Come on, let's get the Veeblax packed away before anything else happens."

As has happened so many times, I left school early that day. I was in an agony of anticipation as we drove back to the embassy, wondering if our principal, Mr. Grand, had already called to discuss the Veeblax incident.

Ms. Buttsman was waiting for us.

"Your Fatherly One wants to see you," she said, raising her left eyebrow. This is a signal I have learned to view with enormous dread.

I took a deep breath. Slowly, nervously, I trudged into the Fatherly One's office.

The news was even worse than I had anticipated.

CHAPTER
6
[L I N N S Y]

Return of the Reporter

Tim and I walked home together the afternoon of the Veeblax disaster. The wind was cold and the sky was gray. Most of the leaves had fallen. A light drizzle began, and I put up my hood to keep my hair dry.

"So, you think there'll be any major fallout from what happened on the playground today?" asked Tim.

"I don't see why there should be," I replied. "Misty wasn't really hurt. I overheard Ms. Weintraub telling McNally that the nurse said she didn't even have any marks from the incident. And it's not like there were any reporters around this time. I'm sure her parents will kick up a fuss. But it shouldn't make the national news or anything."

"I hope you're right," said Tim. "Every time something happens, I'm terrified it's going to ruin Meenom's mission."

I shuddered. What Tim and I knew that most people didn't was that if the peaceful trade mission being run by Pleskit's Fatherly One failed, he would have to leave and let the next Trader who had a claim on the planet take a shot at developing things here. Meenom was trying to create a trade partnership, and treat us like equals. The next Trader might not be so pleasant to deal with. In fact, there was a danger that the next Trader might just take over, colonizing the whole planet the way European countries had once colonized Africa, Asia, and the so-called "New World."

"I'm sure it'll be fine," I said.

Which just goes to show what I know.

When I got up to my apartment (I live two floors above Tim), I saw a pretty redheaded woman leaning against the wall beside my door. "Hi, Linnsy," she said cheerfully. "Got a minute to talk?"

It was Kitty James, the reporter who had done such a nasty job on an interview with Pleskit way back when he first got here. Instantly I was on my guard. The only reason I was willing to talk to her at all was that she had made up for that hatchet job by letting Tim and Pleskit into a TV studio in time to save Meenom from an embarrassing disaster.

"What do you want?" I asked—not very politely, I'm afraid.

"The inside scoop."

"On what?"

Kitty sighed. "Don't play dumb, sweetie. It doesn't suit you. Just tell me about what happened at your school today."

"What makes you think anything happened?" I asked, trying not to sound startled.

Kitty laughed. "Are you kidding? There are two dozen high-tech cameras trained on your building. We can't see what goes on inside, but we sure can spot stuff on the playground, and that little bit with Pleskit's pet today was a doozy. The tape of it is playing all over the world already. But I've got a feeling there was more to the incident than meets the eye, if you know what I mean. And I figure you're the one to tell me about it."

"Why don't you talk to Misty?"

Kitty waved a dismissive hand. "Everyone's going to be talking to her. People will be bored with her face by midnight—though that won't stop those boneheads at the networks from playing the footage over and over again. I want something fresh, kiddo. And I think you can help me get it."

"What you can get is out of here," I said, pushing past her to get into my apartment.

She put out an arm to block me. Leaning close, she whispered, "Think about it, Linnsy. It's always good to have your face on TV."

The weird thing is, normally I would jump at the chance to be on TV. But I've got an ornery streak, and when Kitty said that the first words out of my mouth were, "No, it's not! Now get out of here before I call for help."

"Here," she said. "Take my card. Think it over. Give me a call if you come to your senses. Trang, let's go!"

A muscular Asian man carrying a large video-camera on his shoulder came around the corner.

"Did you just tape us?" I asked angrily.

Trang smiled. He was very handsome. "Nah. I was just waiting in case Kitty needed me."

I watched the two of them go, to make sure they really left. But I was thinking about Misty. I've known her for a long time, and something about the way she had acted just before the incident with the Veeblax was making me a little suspicious.

I went inside. "Did you have a nice day, dear?" called my mother from the kitchen.

"Yeah. Peachy."

"Why don't you come and have some cookies, dear. They're just out of the oven."

"Later, Mom. I've got something I have to do first."

I went to my room and tried to call Misty.

Her line was busy. More reporters, probably.

I flopped down on my bed and started thinking. Misty had looked really smug when she broke through the circle of people around Pleskit to try to take the Veeblax. I knew that look. It means she has a secret.

And later, after she came back from her second visit to the nurse in as many days, she had been unusually quiet, which was totally unlike her.

Misty is hiding something, I thought, *and I'm going to figure out what it is if it's the last thing I ever do.*

CHAPTER
7
[PLESKIT]

Uproar

The Fatherly One was sitting in his command pod, which raises him several feet above the floor. A clear blue shell curves around and over the deeply padded chair, leaving a two-foot wide opening in the front. The armrests are covered by devices that let him enter commands and queries.

The large screen on the wall facing the command pod showed a scene from the wampfields of Hevi-Hevi. The sight of that purple sky made me long for home.

The Fatherly One didn't say anything. He just rolled a knob on his control pad. The scene from Hevi-Hevi vanished, replaced by an Earthly newscast.

To my horror, the entire Misty/Veeblax episode was played out again right in front of my eyes.

"This event was captured by a long-distance videocamera focused on the school," said the Fatherly One. "Even worse, the images I just showed you are currently being broadcast around the world." He tweaked his *sphen-gnut-ksher,* then said sadly, "Pleskit, Pleskit, Pleskit. Will you ever stop bringing me grief?"

I wanted to curl into a ball and *gerdin poozlit.*

"I cannot believe you took the Veeblax to school without clearing it with me first," said the Fatherly One. His voice was sharp now, and I could hear the barely controlled anger.

"You were not available," I said, trying to keep my words clear and unfouled by my fear and sorrow.

"And was it so important for you to take the creature immediately? Was there some emergency that made it impossible to wait for a day or so?"

I hung my head. "No, sir. I have made another error."

When the Fatherly One was done expressing his feelings about my decision to take the Veeblax to school—a process that took nearly a quarter of an hour—I left his office. To my surprise, I found *Wakkam* Akkim waiting for me.

"Do not be downhearted, Pleskit," she said gently, resting the clawlike fingers of her right hand on my shoulder. "Errors are the source of wisdom."

"If that's so, I should be a genius!" I replied.

The *wakkam* shook her head, which caused her feathery brows to wave. "Alas, no. There are thousands of mistakes still to be made!"

This did not make me feel one hundred percent better.

The *wakkam* went in to speak to the Fatherly One. I trudged to the kitchen.

McNally, Barvgis, and Ms. Buttsman were there already, sitting at the table and talking in low tones.

"Another bad one, eh, Pleskit?" said Barvgis. I recognized his tone of voice; it was one he generally saved for the funerals of important galactic leaders.

"I have erred in judgment yet again," I said.

44

"You're not the only one who thinks so," said Barvgis.

The words stung. My reaction must have shown on my face, because Barvgis, who is usually quite kindly, said quickly, "I didn't mean that as a condemnation, Pleskit. Just a statement of fact. We have been listening to the Earthly radio talk shows. You and the Veeblax are the primary topic of conversation." He put up a hand to indicate he needed a second, belched heartily, then continued. "I am amazed at the number of people willing to call in and give an opinion regarding something of which they have no actual knowledge. It seems there are now thousands of Earthlings who consider themselves experts on what happened today."

"Yeah," said McNally, carefully pushing aside the cup of coffee Shhh-foop had given him. "And I've noticed something else, too."

"Which is?" asked Ms. Buttsman.

"Generally speaking, the lower the IQ, the stronger the opinion."

"This appears to be true," said Barvgis. "I have also noticed that the strongest opinions of all seem to be held by radio talk show hosts.

Are they humans, or is there another species on the planet that I was not aware of?"

"You know," said Ms. Buttsman smugly, "the reason I was assigned to the embassy was to help avoid situations such as this. If anyone had bothered to ask, I would have advised against taking the Veeblax to school, which would have saved us from having to endure all this terrible publicity."

"Thank you for that insight, Ms. Buttsman," said McNally coolly.

I tried to eat something, but my *kirgiltum* was in no mood for food. Finally I excused myself and trudged back to my room.

I requested permission from the Fatherly One to stay home from school the next day. Though I have had to leave early several times, this was the first time I had just stayed home since I arrived here. But I did not think I could trust myself. I feared if anyone said something about the Veeblax, I might do something to further endanger the mission.

Late in the afternoon the comm-device I set up with Tim announced an incoming call.

"Call accepted," I said.

Tim's face appeared on the screen. He looked horrible. "Pleskit," he said urgently. "I have to tell you what happened after school today!"

"Is it bad?" I asked, feeling the coldness of *pizumpta* again.

"Bad?" cried Tim. "It's a disaster!"

CHAPTER
8
[TIM]

"Fry the Veeblax!"

When I got to school the morning after the Veeblax incident, swarms of people were blocking the sidewalk. Most of them were carrying protest signs. It reminded me of the way things were when Pleskit first arrived. Only this time the signs were about what had happened on the playground.

As with past demonstrations, there were two main groups. One group called itself We Oppose Men's Evil Nature, or WOMEN for short. As near as I could tell they had decided that the Veeblax latching on to Misty was some kind of anti-girl maneuver. They had several signs that said END

48

HARASSMENT NOW and GIRLS MUST BE SAFE IN SCHOOL. These ideas seemed pretty reasonable to me. I did think the one that said MEN SHOULD BE OUTLAWED was a little over the top. And the one that said JUSTICE FOR MISTY was just plain silly.

Unfortunately, *most* of this group's signs were about the Veeblax itself, and said things like IMPOUND THE VEEBLAX and HARASSMENT BY ANIMALS IS STILL HARASSMENT. The worst one of all said SHOW OUR GIRLS WE CARE! FRY THE VEE-BLAX NOW!

The other group of protesters was from the animal rights group called HEAT (Humans for Ethical Animal Treatment). They were demon-strating on behalf of the Veeblax, which they referred to not as a pet, but as Pleskit's "animal companion." There weren't nearly as many of them, but they were really, really loud.

"Free the Veeblax!" they chanted, which was sort of odd, since it wasn't locked up anywhere.

"*Fry* the Veeblax!" responded the women's rights group furiously.

Next thing you knew people from both sides were charging at each other. It looked like a fight was about to break out, but several cops stepped between them and started dragging people apart. Most of them went peacefully, though one of the women from the animal rights group kept screaming, "You can't touch me, I'm in HEAT!"

I wondered if I could find some other species to be a part of.

Misty herself wasn't in school that day.

Neither was Pleskit. I noticed his desk looked kind of messed up, and wondered if someone had been digging through it for some investigation or something.

Then, as if things weren't bad enough already, Larrabe walked into the classroom, took one look at Harold's cage, and shouted, "Someone stole my woodchuck!"

Of course we all hurried over to the cage, as if by looking at it we could somehow make Harold reappear.

"I don't think anyone really stole him, Larrabe," said Ms. Weintraub.

"Yeah, I hear the market for woodchuck pelts is really down this year," snickered Jordan, which caused Brad Kent to snort in amusement.

Ms. Weintraub shot them a nasty look, then turned back to Larrabe. "It's more likely he escaped somehow," she said soothingly. "Are you sure you closed the top tightly before you went home last night?"

"Positive," said Larrabe, though he didn't look all that positive if you ask me.

"Well, don't worry," said Ms. Weintraub. "I'm sure we'll find him. He's almost certainly still in the school."

Then she had us all make posters to hang up

SIZE - ROUND
EYES - CUTE
FUR - CUDDLY
ANSWERS TO:
• HAROLD
• SNUGELY-
  WUVVY-
  MUFFIN.

HOBBIES INCLUDE:
• Eating
• Sleeping
• Digging
• Being best
  friends with
  Larrabe
  Hicks.

HAVE YOU SEEN THIS WOODCHUCK?

• If found, DO NOT hug, kiss, or show any affection to him on account that he is NOT YOUR WOODCHUCK! No one can love him like Larrabe Hicks.

CONTACT: LARRABE HICKS GEEK BOY!

in the halls, alerting everyone to the fact that we had a missing woodchuck.

We had been working on the posters for about ten minutes when Mr. Grand came in to talk to us. "The governor has assigned a special task force to investigate our school," he said bitterly. "I just want to emphasize here and now that we have zero tolerance for harassment of students. *Zero!*"

He slammed his hand on the desk as he repeated the word, and I got the feeling he almost believed that if he said it loud enough he could make the whole problem go away.

I thought about raising my hand to ask how come Jordan had been allowed to harass me for the last two years, but decided against it.

Mr. Grand glared around at us. I got the feeling he wanted to blame the mess on everyone and everything, and most especially the Veeblax. He made some hints that he wanted to have the poor little guy impounded for the sake of the school, because "we need to show that such things will not be tolerated here," and so on, and so on.

Personally, I wondered how come boneheadedness is considered acceptable in a school, but it was another question I decided not to ask.

It was a long, confusing day, and it only got worse at the end. I had started for home when I realized that I had forgotten my backpack—something I do about three times a week.

I went back to school and headed for our classroom. I was about to go in when I heard Mr. Grand's voice. I stopped to listen. Yeah, I know—it's a bad habit. But if adults didn't keep so much stuff secret from us kids, I would never have developed it to begin with.

"I know you don't like this, Charlotte," he said. "But the superintendent is adamant. He claims there have been too many incidents and it would be better for the class to start fresh."

I felt a wave of coldness shiver through me. *Start fresh?* What was he talking about?

"Andrew, you can't transfer me," said Ms. Weintraub. Her voice was calm but firm. "I haven't done anything wrong. And it would be terrible for the class."

"I don't have any control over the matter, Charlotte. I'm sorry."

He actually did sound sorry, which pretty

much surprised me. But he couldn't have been as sorry as I was. Ms. Weintraub is a great teacher. And what she had said was true: None of the wild and crazy things that had happened since Pleskit got here was her fault.

Actually, some of them were my fault, a fact which gave me an extreme wave of guilt. But a lot of them were also simply because Pleskit was in the room—not that he had done anything wrong, but because powerful forces were trying to cause the Fatherly One's peaceful trade mission to fail.

"I'm going to fight this, Andrew," said Ms. Weintraub. Her voice had changed from firm to fierce. "I'm going to fight it every step of the way. I'll be talking to the union tonight. I'll be talking to the papers. This is my class, and I will *not* let go of them without a fight."

I felt my heart swell. She was the greatest teacher ever. They couldn't transfer her. They just couldn't!

CHAPTER
9
[PLESKIT]

Desperate Decision

After Tim called on Thursday night to tell me that Ms. Weintraub's job was in danger, I couldn't bring myself to go to school again on Friday. I just sat home for a second day and watched as the headlines continued to spin out of control.

They kept playing an interview with Misty where she talked about how terrified she had been when the Veeblax attacked her, and how she felt her "personal space had been violated."

"I've had calls from fifteen heads of state from around the world," said the Fatherly One wearily that afternoon. "Including the president of our host country. They all seem to be much more concerned with what people are saying on the news than with what really happened."

Things were even worse on Saturday.

When we sat down for breakfast on Sunday morning, Barvgis said, "I have noticed that journalism on Earth seems to resemble an adult version of a game the young people play on my planet."

"What game is that, Barv?" asked McNally.

"It's called *Woogdorf K-splah.* It's quite a bit of fun, actually. You choose someone to be It. Then everybody else runs and jumps on top of that person. After a little while they all get off and run and jump on someone else. It doesn't make much sense, but everyone gets to make a lot of noise and use up a lot of energy. As I said, it reminds me of your electronic journalism.

"The big question with *Woogdorf K-splah,*" he continued, shoveling a scoop of *febril-gnurxis* into his mouth, "is whether the being who is It can survive until everyone decides to get off and go chase someone else."

I like Barvgis. But if everyone on his planet is

built the way he is, survival sounded pretty iffy to me.

As if things weren't bad enough without all the huffing and puffing from the news media, Beezle Whompis called me to his desk later that morning and said, "I thought you ought to know that some members of the Trading Federation are taking the uproar about the Veeblax as a sign that your Fatherly One has lost control of the mission and is letting his family affairs affect his work."

"That's not fair!" I said indignantly.

Beezle Whompis laughed, a sound that Tim describes as a radio tuned to the wrong channel. "Fairness has nothing to do with it, Pleskit. You must remember that it is almost certain that your Fatherly One's enemies are feeding exaggerated reports of the situation to the Trader's Council." He paused, then added, "I will say that some of these Traders are walking the fine line between tricky and sneaky."

This was bad news. The Trader's Council is the ruling body of the Trading Federation, and has absolute power.

"Will the Council believe these rascals?" I asked nervously.

Beezle Whompis flickered out of sight, then re-appeared, which is his version of what Earthlings call a *shrug*. "Belief depends on predisposition."

I looked at him blankly. "I don't have the slightest idea what you mean."

"What you already believe affects how you receive new information. Therefore, the council members who are on your Fatherly One's side will tend to discount the false reports. But the ones who have already decided against him will tend to take them seriously."

I asked *Wakkam* Akkim about that later in the day.

"It's accurate as far as it goes," she said, stroking her beaky nose. "But there is more to it than that, Pleskit. Group opinion influences the way people receive information. So does the amount of information. A lie repeated ten times will often have more power than a truth you hear only once."

"That's terrible!" I cried.

"It simply means that you must speak the truth as often as you can," said the *wakkam* calmly. Then she taught me a breathing exercise to help me clear my mind.

"Clear thought is a useful survival tool," she said.

I did feel calm and more clear—until the Fatherly One called me into his office Sunday afternoon for yet another conference.

To my surprise, he climbed out of his command pod and stood directly in front of me.

His eyes were sad, which filled me with terror. Putting his hands on my shoulders, he said, "Pleskit, I have received a call from some officials of our host country's government. They want to take the Veeblax so their scientists can test it to make sure Misty isn't going to catch anything from it."

"They can't do that!" I cried. "The Veeblax did not bite her. It did not harm her in any way. It just clung to her and scared her a little."

"We must accommodate them in some way, Pleskit," said the Fatherly One gently. "The entire mission may depend on it. I have, however, proposed an alternative. We will turn the Veeblax over to a team from the Interplanetary Animal Control Office. They can have someone here by tomorrow morning."

"What difference does that make?" I cried.

59

"Either way they're going to take my pet!"

The Fatherly One looked down. "I thought you might prefer to have the Veeblax go with someone who could do what needs to be done more gently."

His words chilled me, for I knew what they meant.

"Nothing needs to be done!" I cried. "This 'emergency' is political, not medical."

"That may be so, but it's still an emergency caused by your actions!" said the Fatherly One sharply. He stood and turned away. His voice pained, he said, "Pleskit, the Trader's Council has asked—which is their way of demanding—that I do something to quiet this situation. The Animal Control Team will arrive in the morning. I'm sorry, but we must allow them to take the Veeblax."

I broke from his grasp and ran from the room. In my own room I snatched up the Veeblax and held it close. It began to tremble, as if picking up on my fear.

I summoned the air mattress and sat on the edge of it. Then I used *Wakkam* Akkim's breathing technique to avoid slipping into *klep-*

tra. I had to stay calm, stay strong, if not for my sake then for the Veeblax.

I looked down at the little creature. If the Animal Control officers took it I knew I would never see it again. Remorse gripped me. The poor thing was in this trouble because I had made the unwise decision to take it to school. It had not hurt Misty in any way. They were only going to take it because of all the fuss in the news.

The Veeblax, still picking up on my distress, eeped piteously, and shifted so that it looked

younger, with large eyes and rounded features.

This was the shape it took when it was afraid and wanted to be protected, and it pierced my *smorgle*.

I came to a decision. The Veeblax depended on me. Its life was in my hands.

The Animal Control Team was not going to get it, no matter what.

I had been in tough situations before.

I had survived Geembol Seven.

I could survive this world, too.

The Veeblax and I were leaving.

CHAPTER
10
[PLESKIT]

Flight

It is not easy to slip out of the embassy, but not impossible, either. After all, the security devices are designed to keep intruders out, not to keep the staff and residents prisoner.

Also, because it is assumed that I am safe within my own walls, McNally is officially off-duty when I am at home. He has his own living quarters within the embassy, but unless we have events scheduled for the weekend, he is free to come and go as he pleases, and that evening he had chosen to go visit one of his lady friends.

The Fatherly One was tied up with the calls

and messages that continued to flood his office. The other adults in the embassy, though friendly, do not pay much attention to me unless I request it. So, to use the Earthling term, the coast was clear.

My plan was to head for Tim's apartment, with the hope that he could advise me where to travel after that. Unfortunately, I could not call him first on the comm-device to discuss this, since that would leave an electronic trail that would make it too easy for people to follow me.

I decided against taking the Veeblax's carrying case, which was too bulky and awkward for me to travel easily. My pet could walk—preferably in the shape of an Earthling animal, since Tim had already taught it to imitate a cat. If the Veeblax got tired, I would carry it.

I packed a small case for myself, putting in a few pieces of Earth-style clothing and a great deal of Veeblax chow. I hesitated, then threw in a stone from Hevi-Hevi that I had brought with me when we moved here. It was just a plain stone, but it was a piece of home, and I wanted it with me.

I chose my traveling clothes carefully—a dark

outfit with a hood to hide my *sphen-gnut-ksher*. I attached a pull cord to the carrying case, then switched on the case's antigravity device, so that it floated on its own an inch or two above the floor.

I poked my head into the hallway, then glanced up and down to make sure no one was around.

With the Veeblax tucked under my coat, I hurried to the pipe.

Seconds later I was in the garage.

Ralph-the-Driver was polishing the limo, and had his back to me. I slipped past him, then moved silently up the tunnel that leads to the outside, hoping desperately that the Veeblax would not let out a squeak.

At the end of the tunnel I used my *sphen-gnut-ksher* to send a signal that caused the door to slide open. Unlike similar Earthling devices, the door moved in complete silence, for which I was grateful.

I slipped outside, then sent another signal to close the door.

I took a deep breath and stood there, feeling astonished at myself. I had never been out alone on Earth before, much less after dark. The night was colder than I had expected, and the strange smells of this world of which I knew so little were distracting and a little frightening. But it was exhilarating to see the wide sweep of the sky, even if the light of the stars was dimmed by the interference of all the lights from the city.

I tried to spot my home star, but was unable to see it, which depressed me a little. Leaning against the great support hook of the embassy, I practiced *Wakkam* Akkim's breathing technique for a few minutes. When I felt ready I checked to make sure my *sphen-gnut-ksher* was safely tucked under my hood, then started walking.

The embassy is situated on top of a hill in a place called Thorncraft Park. During the day it is usually surrounded—at a distance—by Earthling sightseers. But now, on a cold, dark Sunday night, the hill was deserted.

The Veeblax snuggled against me, a welcome spark of warmth.

I avoided the road at first, but at the base of the hill I had to start walking beside it because otherwise I would not have known how to get to Tim's place.

As the road curved through a wooded area, I was plunged into darkness. I heard a car coming, and scrambled to the side of the road to avoid being seen.

That was when I heard the snuffling sound for the first time. It came from the trees off to my right.

A moment later a horrible odor assaulted me.

Frightened, I began to run, stumbling through the trees, clutching the Veeblax, trying not to let go of my travel case.

I could hear something big crashing and thrashing along behind me. As I ran my mind was racing, too, trying to remember what I had learned of Earthling animals, to imagine what could possibly be following me through the night.

I tripped on a root. The Veeblax squealed in terror, though whether it was afraid of what was following us or simply frightened by my fall, I was not certain.

At last I made it back to the road, where I continued to run as fast as I could. When I left the wooded area, the sound of pursuit stopped, as if the creature—whatever it was—would not leave the trees.

I trotted on, sore and exhausted from the run. Though I could no longer hear my pursuer, I continued to glance behind me. Once I thought I saw a large form in the moonlight. (And how odd it seemed to have only one moon!) I began to move faster again, and when I looked back, it was gone.

Suddenly I realized I had lost track of where I was. Panic seized me. I had been out of the embassy for less than an hour, and already I was lost.

Cars whizzed past, unbelievably loud and smelly. The horrible fumes made me stagger in disgust, and I wondered how the Earthlings can stand to live with such a stench.

The Veeblax shrieked in terror each time a car went by.

"Shhhh!" I urged, stroking its back. "Please, you have to be quiet!"

I pressed it against me more tightly. It buried its face against my neck, which muffled the sounds of its fear.

I trudged on, desperately seeking something that I recognized. At last I spotted a street I knew from our drive to school.

Feeling much relieved, I began to run again.

It was only when I arrived at Tim's door that I realized what a difficult situation I was about to put him in.

But I had nowhere else to turn.

Even so, I stood in the hall in front of his apartment door for some time, trying to decide whether to knock, or turn and flee back into the darkness.

CHAPTER
11

[L I N N S Y]

Search Party

I spent most of Sunday watching the news, which I found fascinating the way some people find a car wreck fascinating. I was so sick of seeing Misty's whiny face that I wanted to puke. It seemed as if her experience with the Veeblax—or, at least, her memory of it— became more horrifying with every new interview.

What finally made me turn off the TV in disgust was when I saw her tell one interviewer, "Yes, Barbara, I truly thought I was going to die."

Actually, it wasn't her words that got to me as much as it was the trembling lip and the single tear rolling down her cheek. Misty had been using that trick since kindergarten, and most of our teachers caught on to it by the second week of each school year.

Now the entire world seemed to be taking it seriously!

I went to my room. I was working on the final draft of my poem for Percy, which I had titled "The Death of Truth," when my mother knocked at my door and said, "Mr. Timothy is here to see you, honey. He seems to think it's urgent."

I sighed. "Everything is urgent for Tim, Mom."

But I went to see what he wanted.

"I have to talk to you," he hissed, not coming into the apartment.

"About what?"

He made a motion with his head to indicate he wanted me to step outside. I sighed, then shouted, "Back in a minute, Mom!"

"All right," I said, once I was in the hall. "What is it?"

"Pleskit's run away. He's in my apartment right now. *With* the Veeblax."

"He can't do that!" I cried.

"He already has. The question is, what do we do about it?"

"What did your mother say?"

"She's at work. The hospital's got her on the night shift this month."

I thought for a minute, then said, "All right, I'd better come down there. Give me a second to clear things with my parents."

I told Mom I had to help Tim with an emergency. Since Tim's life is a constant emergency, this didn't get her all that worried.

Tim and I hurried down to his apartment. Pleskit was sitting in the living room, looking totally miserable. The Veeblax lay next to him, looking like a melted candle.

"Poor baby," I said, scooping it into my arms.

Pleskit smiled. I felt really sorry for him—and even sorrier when he said, "An animal control team is coming to take the Veeblax away. I do not believe it will survive the tests they intend to do on it. I cannot let this happen!"

Before we could discuss what he should do next, someone rang the buzzer.

Tim tiptoed to the door and looked through the peephole. When he turned back to me and Pleskit, his face was white. "It's McNally!" he whispered urgently. "What should I say?"

I hurried over to join him. "Don't say anything. Pretend we're not here."

"Tim!" shouted McNally, pounding on the door again. "Come on, Tim. I know you're in there! Let me in!"

"I can't," said Tim. "My mother doesn't allow me to open the door for strangers when she's not here."

"I'm no stranger!" shouted McNally furiously.

Before Tim could answer, we heard another voice. "Federal Marshals!" it bellowed. "We've got a search warrant. Open up or we're coming in anyway."

Tim looked at me. His eyes were wide. I recognized the look. It wasn't fear, it was excitement.

"Get Pleskit out on the fire escape," he whispered. "Hurry!"

I scurried back into the living room. "This way," I said to Pleskit, taking him by the hand and leading him to the window. "Make sure you've got everything. We'll come get you as soon as they're gone."

"Open up!" bellowed the guy at the door.

"The lock's stuck!" shouted Tim.

"Open this door or there won't be a lock, kid!"

Veeblax clinging to his neck, Pleskit climbed out the window. I turned back and gasped. His travel case was still on the floor. Well, actually, it was floating a couple of inches above the floor. I grabbed it and thrust it toward the window. It floated over the edge.

"Hold on, guys!" shouted Tim, rattling the lock mechanism as if he was actually working on it. "I've almost got it."

I pulled the window down, then hurried to Tim's side. "All clear," I whispered.

He opened the door, crying, "Got it! Whew. Sorry about the trouble, guys."

McNally started to come through but was muscled aside by another man, dressed all in black. Two other guys came in right after him.

The lead guy held out a badge and said, "All right, where's the alien?"

"How should I know?" asked Tim.

"Look, buster—just tell me where he is, and this will be easier for both of us."

"Hey, lay off," said McNally, who had pushed in after the marshals. "They're only kids."

"Kids who may be involved in an interplanetary diplomatic crisis," replied the lead marshal. "Now shut up, McNally, if you don't want to lose your job—which you might anyway for letting that kid get away."

McNally set his jaw. "I was off duty when Pleskit disappeared. Anyway, my job isn't to protect him when he's in the embassy, it's to protect him when he's out in the world."

"Well, he's out in the world now, smart guy, so just shut up."

McNally looked furious but didn't say anything else.

The marshals started a search of Tim's apartment, looking in every closet, under every bed, in every drawer, even in places where Pleskit couldn't possibly fit. One of them opened a doorway in the hall, then quickly flattened himself against the wall. He pulled out a gun and stretched his neck so he could peer around the doorframe. Then he jumped into the doorway and began to swing the gun back and forth. "If there's anyone in there, freeze!" he roared.

"What is it, Croydon?" called the head marshal.

"I'm not sure, Parker. I think there was some sort of struggle here. Maybe an abduction attempt. You'd better come take a look."

I burst out laughing.

"You!" said Parker. "What's so funny?"

"That's Tim's room," I said, trying to stifle my laughter. "It always looks like that!"

The agents scowled at me, then Parker and Croydon waded into the room (*wading* is the only word that properly describes what it's like trying to cross Tim's floor), leaving the third guy in the hall to keep an eye on me and Tim.

It didn't do them any good. They found no sign of either Pleskit or the Veeblax.

Parker and Croydon came out of the room, looking cranky and disgusted.

"You know, you guys," said Tim, "my mother's not going to like this."

"Yeah, well the Board of Health wouldn't like what we just saw," growled Parker. "Now shut up, unless you're ready to tell me where your little purple pal has gotten to." He turned to look around the room, then smiled. "Never mind. I think I just figured it out!"

I barely restrained my gasp as he walked to the window where I had let Pleskit out. It was open just a crack, letting in cold air. Parker shoved it all way open, then climbed out onto the fire escape. Sticking his head back into the room he said, "Croydon, you come with me. Havelitz, you stay here and keep an eye on those two. Might as well keep an eye on McNally while you're at it."

McNally muttered something. I think it was probably just as well I couldn't make out the exact words.

I was terrified for Pleskit and the Veeblax— not to mention for me and Tim. The next five minutes were the slowest of my life.

I know it was five minutes because I could see the clock on the kitchen wall from where I stood.

But when Parker and Croydon came back

through the window, they didn't have Pleskit with them.

"Where's the kid?" asked Havelitz.

"Wherever he is, it's not out there," said Parker angrily. "There's a gate at the bottom of the escape and the latch is jammed—which is going to mean a safety citation for this building if nothing else."

"We scoured the top of the building," added Croydon. "I guarantee you, he's nowhere up there."

Parker turned to Tim. "All right, this is your last chance, kid. Where's the alien?"

"I don't have the slightest idea," said Tim, looking extremely worried. "And I *really* wish I knew."

CHAPTER
12
[PLESKIT]

Over the Edge

No sooner had Linnsy shoved me out the window onto the fire escape than I heard her scurry back to the front door.

The Veeblax still clinging to my neck, I slipped to the side, climbed a couple of steps, then leaned back to peer through the top corner of the window. I pulled back quickly as I saw a gang of federal agents burst into the room.

I felt like a criminal.

I raced up the fire escape to the roof, hoping desperately that I had not accidentally left any sign of my presence back in Tim's living room.

The air was cold, the sky clear and bright with stars. I lay on my back, staring up at them and wishing that I had the ability to fly back out there, far from this planet where I seemed to get in trouble no matter what I did.

A light wind began to blow and the cold became more intense. I huddled in on myself for warmth. And as I hunched there, quivering in the cold and the dark, I understood that I had done the wrong thing in coming here to Tim's.

We have a proverb on Hevi-Hevi: "Bring not trouble to the homes of your friends."

But that was exactly what I had done.

I knew Tim was glad to shelter me. Was he not my friend? But I also realized I should have expected that McNally would come here to look for me. I don't know if I should have expected the government agents, but I had to admit to myself that if I thought about it, their arrival wasn't all that surprising.

I knew one more thing: Even if the agents left now, the odds that they would come back were very high.

Almost as high as I was here on the roof.

For that matter, the odds were very good that

they would soon figure out I had used the fire escape, and come up here after me.

The thought seized me like a *kalyap*. I had to get away from here!

But how?

I hurried back to the fire escape. If I went down that way, the agents were likely to spot me passing the window.

I hurried across the roof to the front of the building and looked over the edge. The limo was down there, as well as two other large, dark cars. Each had a man in a black suit lounging against it.

I could only see one way out. It was a desperate gamble, but this was a desperate situation.

Cradling the Veeblax in my arms, I went to the back corner of the building. I peered over.

It was a long way down.

I tucked the Veeblax into my coat and fastened it tightly. That wouldn't hold it if it really wanted to get out, of course, since it could simply change shape and slither away. But I had trained it to stay put in a situation like this.

I got my travel case and placed it on the edge of the building, which was about a foot higher than the roof itself. Then I climbed onto the case and wrapped the strap over my legs. I fastened it back to the case, tightened my legs, gripped the handle as tightly as I could with my left hand.

Then I cranked the antigrav device up to its highest setting, and pushed myself off the building.

The wind whistled past my ears as we hurtled through the darkness and cold to the ground so far below. I knew the antigrav device wouldn't really kick in until we were about thirty feet from ground level. Even so, the first fifty feet of that fall were sheer terror.

The Veeblax flattened against me, wailing piteously.

My *sphen-gnut-ksher* was sparking out of control.

Suddenly our rate of descent began to decrease. It had only taken seconds—actually, I calculated it out at 2.3 seconds—but it had felt like an eternity.

At about ten feet from the ground the case slowed to a drift.

At about four feet it stopped altogether, and I

had to adjust the control so it would settle all the way down and we could climb off.

I took a deep breath. We had survived.

I glanced around. Behind Tim's apartment building is a little wooded area. It was the perfect place to take shelter while I tried to decide what to do next. Still clutching the Veeblax, I scurried toward the woods, hoping desperately that none of the agents had seen me make my escape.

We stopped beneath a tree at the edge of the woods, and I looked back at the building. I was torn between glee and horror over what I had just done.

Then I turned my back on the building and walked to the center of the little forest. I sat beneath a tree and began trying to think of where to go now. But it's not easy to hide when you're the only purple kid on the planet.

I was going to need help.

All right, who besides Tim was apt to be sympathetic? I needed someone who would understand my situation. Someone who could see things from a different angle.

Someone who could sympathize with an alien.

But who on Earth would that be?

And then, suddenly, I had the answer.

I waited in the woods until I was pretty sure the people searching for me had gone. Then I made my way to a phone booth, hoping desperately that I could find the right number, that the person I wanted would be home, and most of all, that he would be willing to take the risk of sheltering a runaway alien.

CHAPTER
13
[PLESKIT]

Secret Hideout

It was approaching midnight when I made my way to the edge of town, and the streets were almost completely empty. The cold was beginning to bother me, but it was also making the Veeblax sleepy, which made it easier to carry.

Finally I reached the corner I was looking for. I glanced around. There was no one in sight. Even so, I found a dark doorway to shelter in.

After a while—it seemed hours, but I know it was less—a dark blue car, somewhat old and battered looking, pulled up to the curb. The

window rolled down. A hand reached out and slapped the side of the car three times.

Clutching the Veeblax, pulling my carrying case, I scurried to the passenger side.

Percy the Mad Poet opened the door and let me in.

"Thank you," I said breathlessly.

"I don't know why I'm doing this," Percy replied as I buckled my seat belt. "Are you sure they won't zap my brain for hiding you?"

"I do not feel certain about anything at the moment," I said.

"Well, that's comforting," said Percy. "Come on, let's get you somewhere warm. This is my daughter, Pandora," he added, gesturing to the backseat.

I turned to look. The girl sitting in back was tiny and fragile looking, but quite attractive by Earthling standards, with a turned-up nose and large eyes.

"Hi, Pleskit," she said shyly, giving me a little wave.

I waved back. "Hi," I said.

Then I leaned against the seat and closed my eyes. I was totally exhausted.

*   *   *

Percy and Pandora lived about fifteen miles out of Syracuse, in a rugged, hilly area that was very isolated. The last part of the trip took us over a dirt road.

I was amazed at how much an Earth vehicle can bounce.

Their house was small but comfortable. They had a wood-burning stove that I found very charming, and two large dogs named Keats and Shelley that both the Veeblax and I found quite alarming.

After Percy had given me something warm to drink, we talked a little about what was going on. Then he said, "Come on, kid, I've got a spot where they'll never find you."

I followed him out of the house, along a little path through the woods, to a small metal structure on wheels.

"This trailer is my writing hideaway," said Percy. "I don't let many people in here. But this is a special occasion."

The trailer was on the edge of a cliff, so that the back side of it had an open view of the sky and of the city far below. I found it very beautiful, and more peaceful than anywhere else I had been on Earth.

Percy put a brown stick in his mouth and set the end of it on fire. Except it didn't blaze, just glowed a little. He began to puff on it, blowing out clouds of smoke.

"What is that thing?" I cried in horror.

Percy looked startled. "Just a cigar," he said. "Oh. Sorry. I forgot how much they bother some people. That's why I come out here to smoke 'em. Just lit up by habit."

"Oh, well, that's all right," I said. "For a moment I feared that this was really a trap and you were trying to kill me or something."

"Hey, kid, I'm probably risking my life to shelter you like this!"

I looked at him curiously. "For some reason I thought you would help me. And I was right, though I am still not sure what made me think so. Why are you willing to take this risk?"

Percy shrugged. "Anyone who tries to make his living as a poet in America has to be a little bit of an outlaw. And since it's partly my fault that you brought the Veeblax to school, I feel responsible. I've been following this story in the papers, and I think you're getting a bum rap. It's all hysteria and nonsense. But I suspect the dust will settle after a while and people will get over being hysterical about the Veeblax. At least, I hope so. Until then, you need a place to hide."

He paused, raised his cigar, realized that he had put it out, stared at the end of it for a second, and then said, "Look, Pleskit, I may be a poet and an outlaw, but I'm also a parent. So I know something of what your Fatherly One is going through right now. We've got to get a message to him so that he'll know you're safe."

I did not want to hear this. I was angry at the Fatherly One for agreeing to surrender the Veeblax. But I knew Percy was right. So I wrote a short note saying that I was safe and asking him not to look for me (a request that I knew he would ignore) and handed it to Percy.

"I'll drive Pandora back into town and let her slip it under the door of Tim's apartment," he said, tucking it into his pocket. "That way if someone happens to spot her, they still won't know where it came from."

I watched the poet go back up the trail toward his little house.

I was all alone in the woods of a world that was still quite strange and alien to me.

I crawled into the little bed at one end of the trailer. Cuddling the Veeblax to my chest, I tried to sleep.

I was almost out when I heard something snuffling around outside the trailer.

As the snuffling continued, I realized how truly alone I was. Because the trailer was Percy's place for being isolated, he did not have a telephone here, so there was no way for me to even call him at the house.

Then I remembered that he wasn't at the house anyway; he had driven back into town to deliver my note.

I tried to remember what I knew of Earthling wildlife. I did not think there were any large and dangerous creatures in this part of the planet. Well, except human beings, of course.

Snuffle. Snuffle.

"Go away!" I yelled, banging on the side of the trailer.

Whatever was out there emitted a loud, shrill whistle. This was followed by an enormous sound that reminded me of . . . well, it sounded like a giant fart, though not one that had any meaning.

A horrible odor drifted into the trailer.

But whatever had been snuffling around outside was gone.

Even so, it was a long time before I finally fell asleep.

CHAPTER
14
[TIM]

Missing: One Alien

School on Monday was dreadful. Aside from the fact that there were more protesters outside the building than ever (at least the cops kept them a decent distance from the school grounds), Ms. Weintraub looked tired and unhappy. I was pretty sure it was because she was in danger of being transferred out of our class. And I couldn't say anything about it because I wasn't supposed to know.

Larrabe was in mourning because Harold was still missing.

Linnsy and I had been warned to keep our mouths shut about Pleskit being in a similar condition. We probably would have anyway, since it was clear that the embassy was sitting on the news, and we didn't want to be the ones to spill it.

"I'm sorry to see that Pleskit and Misty are not here this morning," said Ms. Weintraub as she took attendance. "I do hope it's not because of all the trouble about the Veeblax."

It was one of the sillier things I've ever heard her say, since we all knew that was exactly why they weren't there.

The day dragged on. Shortly before lunchtime the class phone rang. Ms. Weintraub picked it up, listened for a moment, then turned to me and said, "Tim, you're wanted in the office."

"Nice to know he's wanted somewhere," said Jordan.

Brad Kent's snicker was cut off by Ms. Weintraub's patented glare o' doom. She turned back to me. "You'd better go, Tim," she said gently.

Filled with dread, wondering what I had done now, I trudged out of the room.

Mr. Grand was waiting in front of his office.

"There's someone here to see you," he said.

He took me into the conference room next to his office.

My dread grew deeper. Sitting at the table was Pleskit's Fatherly One.

Mr. Grand stepped quietly out of the room. Meenom motioned for me to sit down across from him.

"I need to talk with you, Tim," he said. His voice was firm, but filled with sorrow.

I gulped. "Yes, sir."

He folded his purple hands in front of him. "Since McNally came to visit you last night, I know that you are aware Pleskit is missing, something we have otherwise kept secret. You and I have talked seriously before, Tim. And I have saved you from big trouble on at least one occasion, when you were hiding in my office."

I considered pointing out that I had saved him from big trouble at least once, too, but decided against it.

"I want to know if you have any idea where he is."

"No, sir, I don't," I said.

He leaned forward. "Have you seen him since he disappeared?"

I hesitated. I didn't want to rat on my friend. On the other hand, I couldn't actually tell where he was, since I didn't know. And I was very worried about what might have happened to him.

"He came to my apartment for a while last night," I said, trying to figure out how to tell this without getting Linnsy in trouble, too. "But he slipped out during the night without . . . without telling me where he was going."

Meenom sighed.

"He was awfully upset, sir," I said. "He's afraid of what's going to happen to the Veeblax, and he feels totally guilty about it. But he also thinks it's completely unfair. I do, too, for that matter."

I sat back and blushed; I had said more than I intended.

"It probably *is* unfair," said Meenom quietly. "But one of the things my childling has to learn—and, I think, you as well, Tim—is that life is not always fair. I wish it could be. I wish I could go back to the time in my own life when I thought it was possible. I do not want to see the

Veeblax taken from him. I do not want the creature to be hurt. But there is a great deal at stake
here, Tim. A great deal."

He stood up. Then he reached into his robe
and withdrew a shiny purple object about the
size of a yo-yo. It had the symbol of the Hevi-
Hevian embassy engraved on the top.

He held it between his hands and gave it a
slight twist. The top flipped back, revealing a
tiny screen.

"You can use this to contact me if you learn anything about Pleskit's location," he said.

He showed me how to work the thing.

Then he left, looking so sad and worried I might even have told him where Pleskit was—if I had had any idea myself.

CHAPTER
15

POINTS OF VIEW

HEADLINES AND OPENING PARAGRAPHS FROM NEWS ARTICLES COLLECTED BY MS. WEINTRAUB'S CLASS FOR THEIR CURRENT EVENTS BULLETIN BOARD:

From *The Weekly World Watchdog*:

ALIEN BOY'S PET A MENACE TO EARTH SECURITY

This week there was a terrifying incident in Syracuse, New York, where the alien embassy is headquartered. Pleskit Meenom, son of Hevi-Hevian ambassador Meenom Ventrah, took his pet Viblex to school with him. The vicious creature attached itself to a helpless schoolgirl, who was nearly strangled before they could pull it off her. In the end it was Robert McNulty, the alien's bodyguard, who valiantly wrenched the creature away, at great personal risk to his own safety, thereby saving the helpless girl's life.

Outraged citizen's have demanded that the creature be seized and examined to discover if there is any threat to the girls' life.

From the *New York Scribe:*

GIRL ATTACKED BY ALIEN MENACE

(Dateline: Syracuse)

An unsettling incident in this small upstate city has had national, international, and perhaps even interplanetary reverberations.

Pleskit Meenom, son of the Hevi-Hevian ambassador Meenom Ventrah, took his pet Veeblax to school last week as part of a class poetry project, started by avant-garde poet Percy Canterfield. When the creature attached itself to one of the boy's classmates, it started a furor that has pitted women's rights activists, who see the attack as an act of sexual harassment, against animal rights activists, particularly those in HEAT (Humans for Ethical Animal Treatment), who consider calls for the Veeblax to be impounded as an act of what they call "species-based colonialism."

From the on-line newsletter of We Oppose Men's Evil Nature (WOMEN):

ALIEN MEN NO DIFFERENT THAN EARTH PIGS
SAYS WOMEN'S GROUP

Women around the world were outraged to learn of the way the alien boy currently attending school on Earth used his so-called pet to assault a helpless girl on the schoolyard grounds this week.

Is there to be no end to the outrages perpetrated on women by the male hegemony? It is clear that sexism is a problem that extends throughout the entire galaxy.

From a fundraising letter for Humans for Ethical
Animal Treatment:

EARTHLING INTOLERANCE ENDANGERS ALIEN PET

Once again our human-centric view of life has
endangered the welfare of an innocent creature.
The animal companion of the alien boy Pleskit
Meenom has been the subject of a vicious cam-
paign of hate and lies since the unfortunate incident wherein a schoolgirl recklessly provoked
the animal into an attack that is now being used
as an excuse to call for the animal's death. We in
HEAT condemn this as a clear act of human
chauvinism.

CHAPTER
16
[PLESKIT]

On the Road Again

On Monday morning I was roused by the light filtering through the trailer's dirt-streaked windows.

My *kirgiltum* felt empty, and I wondered if Percy was going to bring me some breakfast.

Alone in the trailer, I had little to do except play with the Veeblax. Though I did not mean to pry, I began to leaf through the papers on Percy's desk. As I did, I found the following poem:

"Alien in Hiding"
by
Percy Canterfield

No matter how much I try to be like the others
I cannot.
My difference shrieks its way to the surface
It is not my skin
My face
My hands
That set me apart.
It is who I am,
More different than anyone has ever dreamed
    of being.
Me only.
Me alone.
Me.
The alien.
The stargazer.
The lost boy.

It is hard to explain how this made me feel.
Part of me was warmed by the idea that someone understood so well how I felt. Another part
was annoyed that Percy was writing about my

private situation, putting my intimate feelings on paper.

So I was a little embarrassed when he came in later and noticed that the poem was on top of the stack. "Oh, did you read that one?" he asked. "I wrote it four years ago. Always been one of my favorites."

"You mean it's *not* about me?" I asked in surprise.

Percy looked as surprised as I felt. Then a light of recognition went on in his eyes and he laughed. "Heh. It does look like it's about you, doesn't it, Pleskit? Sorry, though. It's just something I wrote one day when I was feeling lonely. In this culture it's pretty easy for a poet to feel as if he came from another planet."

Then he invited me and the Veeblax to come up to the house for some breakfast.

Pandora was already at the table when I came in.

"Isn't it Monday?" I asked, feeling a little confused.

"All day long," said Percy, going to the stove to get a big blue pot. Whatever was in it smelled most enticing.

I turned to Pandora. "Don't you have to be in school?"

She smiled. "Daddy said I should stay home so I don't accidentally give you away."

"Seemed easier that way," said Percy with a shrug when I glanced at him. He poured a black liquid out of the pot into a big mug sitting in front of me.

"What's this?" I asked.

"Coffee," said Percy. Then he blinked and said, "Sorry. I probably should have asked if you drink the stuff."

"My bodyguard McNally likes coffee. Shhh-foop, our Queen of the Kitchen, tries to make it for him, but it never seems to come out right." I sniffed the black brew. "It smells wonderful."

Pandora made a face. "Smells better than it tastes," she said. "I think it's yucky!"

I took a sip, then coughed and said, "Pandora's right."

Percy laughed. "It's an acquired taste. Here, have some oatmeal."

Pandora showed me how to put on brown

sugar and milk. It tasted very good, even reminded me a little of *febril gnurxis*, which is my favorite morning food.

After breakfast Percy took me for a long walk in the woods. I loved the way the fallen leaves crackled beneath our feet, and even more the wonderful smell that they released as we stirred them up.

If I had not been so torn with worry, it would have been one of my better days on Earth. But as the day went on, I realized that I was putting Percy and his daughter in danger by asking them to hide me. I couldn't stay here forever. In fact, I wasn't sure where I could stay. Maybe I would just have to keep running.

It grew dark around six o'clock. We had a pleasant supper in the little house. But I was feeling restless because I knew that I could not stay.

Back in the little trailer I wrote a note for Percy, thanking him for all he had done to help, and explaining why I was leaving. I packed my things, including my last bag of Veeblax chow. Then, yet again, I slipped away without telling anyone where I was going—which was sort of getting to be a habit with me.

My plan for the time being was a bold one. I was going to the school, on the theory that it was the last place that anyone would look for me. I even had the perfect place there to hide—my Personal Needs Chamber, which was kept locked, since I was the only one who used it.

I made a wide circle around Percy's house, using the lights from its windows to guide me. I had almost made it back to the little dirt road when I heard that snuffling sound again.

I wanted to shout for whatever it was to go away, but didn't dare. So I threw a stick, hissing, "Leave me alone!"

The sound stopped.

I started down the road. Five or ten minutes later I heard it again, in the woods off to my right.

"Go away!" I shouted, confident that I was far enough from the house that Percy and Pandora would not hear me this time.

Again the noise stopped. That was good. But

it was a long walk down Percy's steep dirt road, and I could tell that I was being followed the entire distance. The journey was long and difficult enough as it was. I would have been much happier without having to also endure the fear that whatever was following me would finally get up the courage to approach me more closely.

Once I reached the main road, I could no longer hear the creature following me, and I felt much better.

There were not many cars at first, but as I got closer to the city, that changed. I had to keep ducking off to the side to avoid being seen, which slowed me down a great deal.

By the time I finally reached the school, it was a little after nine according to the clock on the front of the building.

To my relief, the school was dark. The doors were locked, of course, but I was able to use the energy from my *sphen-gnut-ksher* to get one open.

Even though the building was empty, I walked carefully and quietly down the hall to my Personal Needs Chamber.

It was pretty spooky inside the school at night, with no one there.

Then, as I was opening the door to my Personal Needs Chamber, someone tapped me on the shoulder, nearly causing me to *deefrim* in terror.

CHAPTER
17
[LINNSY]

Misty's Secret

Monday afternoon, instead of going straight home, I walked over to Misty's neighborhood. For a while I just stood on the corner of Oak and Ash, staring at Misty's house. Then I took a deep breath and walked up the sidewalk to her front door.

I had decided that if we were going to put an end to the nonsense about the Veeblax being a predator, I had to get Misty on our side. I hoped that if she just said she wasn't really all that upset, things might settle down and we could get back to normal.

I don't go to visit Misty all that often these

days. The two of us haven't been all that close since the time in third grade when she spread a nasty rumor about me and Brad Kent. We got over it, after a while, and got along okay in school and at parties and stuff. But we were never really friends after that.

I rang the bell.

After a few minutes I heard someone come to the door. The door didn't open, though. Instead, a voice shouted, "If you're a reporter, go away!"

"Misty, it's me—Linnsy!"

"Go away anyway."

"Misty!"

"I mean it!"

"Misty, I have to talk to you."

"About what?"

"Pleskit. And the Veeblax."

"I don't want to talk."

"Misty, if you don't open that door and talk to me, I'm going to tell Chris Mellblom who *really* sent him that love note last month."

The door swung open.

"What do you want?" she said sullenly.

"I just want to talk," I said. "I'm trying to get this whole situation with you and Pleskit and the Veeblax figured out, and I need some details."

She stepped aside and let me come in. She looked as if she had been crying.

"What's wrong?" I asked.

"Nothing. What do you want?"

"I just want to know a little bit more about what happened that day with the Veeblax."

She shifted her eyes sideways, and my suspicion meter, which was already quivering, jumped right over the edge. I've known Misty since first grade, and I know how she acts when she's trying to hide something, or when she's feeling guilty.

"Was it really as scary as it seemed?" I asked, trying not to sound suspicious.

She hesitated, then shook her head. "No, not really."

I blinked, trying to look more surprised than I really felt. "But you talked like it was horrible!" I said.

She got up and walked away, then came back, then walked away again. I didn't say anything, just sat and waited. Misty can't stand silence, so if you don't say anything, she usually will start talking, just to fill the gap.

"Well, it really was a little scary," she said. "But I was feeling okay by the time I got home. But then the reporters came to talk to me about it, and they kept trying to make me feel like I had been more scared than I really was. Pretty soon I started thinking maybe I had been. And the more scared I acted, the better they liked it."

"You mean they were trying to get you to exaggerate the way you felt?"

She nodded her head. "One of them said that the more upset I looked, the more times she could get the television to run my picture."

I was furious, though whether I was madder at Misty or the reporter, I still couldn't say. It made me sick to think that they can put stuff like that on the air and call it news and pretend they're showing the truth.

I wanted to shake her, to say, "Do you know how much trouble you caused for Pleskit with all this?" Only I didn't, because I knew she would stop talking if I did.

I'm glad I kept my cool, because after I had talked to her long enough, and pointed out that Pleskit was missing and for all we knew he might be dead, and that the Veeblax might still die, even if they found him, all because of what happened on the playground, she burst into tears.

"I can't stand it!" she cried. "I'm such a horrible person."

"What are you talking about?" I asked in alarm.

Which was when I finally found out the real reason that the Veeblax had glommed onto her that day.

CHAPTER
18
[TIM]

Beast!

On Monday night Mom had just left for the hospital and I was just putting the last of the dishes into the dishwasher when the phone rang.

I picked up the receiver. A small, girlish voice said, "Is this Tim Tompkins?"

"Yeah. Who is this?"

"I can't tell you. But I have to let you know that your friend Pleskit was staying at my house. I'm calling because he left without telling us. I wanted to let you to know that he was fine until an hour or so ago, but that now we don't know where he is. My daddy is out looking for him. He said to call you to let you know."

"Who are you?" I cried. *"Where* are you?"

I heard nothing but a click, and then silence.

Heart pounding, I sat down to think. Pleskit was all right—or had been, until just a little while ago. That was good news. But he was on the road again, and that was bad news. Where could he be going? And who had he been staying with?

I got out a pad and paper and started to make a list of places outside the embassy that Pleskit knew well.

I could only think of one.

The school.

I grabbed my coat and bolted out of the apartment, down to the basement where I store my bike. I unlocked my bike, sighed at my own forgetfulness, and raced back up to the apartment to get a flashlight.

Back down the stairs again. Once I was out of the apartment, it took me only about five minutes to get to the school.

The place was dark and deserted looking. I

knew it would be locked up, but I also suspected Pleskit might have some high-tech way
of getting past any locks.

I leaned my bike against the side wall and
started to make a slow circle of the school. I
mostly kept my flashlight off, using it only
when I had to.

The first door I tried was locked. So was the
second. But the third, one of the side doors,
was wide open. This struck me as being strange,
but it was also a sign that Pleskit might have
gone in.

Still, it wasn't like him to leave something
like that open, which made me wonder if he
was all right.

I noticed an unpleasant odor as I walked in,
and wondered if Pleskit had some special fart
he made when he was particularly afraid. I
thought I heard something at the far end of the
hall, down toward our classroom. I stopped,
held my breath, listening.

Nothing.

Then I heard a noise in the other direction,
toward Pleskit's Personal Needs Chamber.

Flicking off my flashlight, I began tiptoeing

in that direction, moving cautiously, just in case it *wasn't* him.

It was. He was just opening the door to the chamber.

Maybe I should have shouted for him. But I was afraid that if I did, he would run and try to escape. So I slipped up quietly and put my hand on his shoulder. This was probably a mistake, since it caused him to screech and jump in surprise. The Veeblax shrieked, too. Pleskit began to tremble, and for an instant I was afraid that he was going to go into *kleptra*. But finally he took a deep breath, then said, "What are you doing here?"

"Looking for you!"

"Please go away. Pretend you have not seen me."

He seemed so desperate and frightened it nearly broke my heart. But I was angry, too. We were supposed to be friends, and he had run off without telling me where he was going.

"Pleskit, everyone is worried about you. Your Fatherly One is just about out of his mind."

His face had a hard, desperate look I had

never seen before. "I am not going to let them take the Veeblax, Tim. You have not had a pet, so maybe you do not understand—"

"I understand!" I snapped angrily. "All right, at least let me show you a better place to hide. Don't forget, I've spent a fair amount of time scoping this place out for spots where I could get away from Jordan."

But as we started toward the spot I had in mind, we heard a sound from behind us.

We turned—and screamed.

An enormous pile of fur was lurching toward us. It reared on its hind legs. Its head nearly scraped the ceiling. It had blazing red eyes and its breath smelled like fresh vomit.

Then it farted, releasing a horrible pink and orange gas that swirled around it like a cloud.

The smell was even worse than its breath.

"What is it?" shrieked Pleskit, coughing and choking.

"I'm not sure," I gasped. "But it looks like . . . Harold!"

The giant woodchuck thing emitted a horrible, high-pitched whistle as it lurched toward us again.

The Veeblax eeped in terror.

Pleskit and I turned and ran, screaming as we went.

The sound of the woodchuck's enormous paws scrabbling on the tile was horribly close behind us.

CHAPTER
19
[PLESKIT]

Animal Control

As Tim and I raced down the hall to escape the monster woodchuck, my mind was racing, too. This had to be the same creature that had been following me for the last two days.

But could it really be Larrabe's sweet little woodchuck?

If so, what had happened to make it grow like this? And, even more pressing, why had it been following me?

We reached a corner, and in my haste I stumbled and fell. The woodchuck was only a few feet away. I thought my doom was upon me, but the Veeblax flung itself in front of me.

Stretching itself up in a terrible shape, it uttered a piercing squeal that caused Harold to draw back.

Tim grabbed my hand and dragged me to my feet. I grabbed the Veeblax and we ran on, but it was only seconds before we again heard the giant paws scrabbling close behind us. Then, suddenly, the sound stopped. I glanced over my shoulder. Harold was standing still. He looked worried. He closed his eyes and we heard a sudden ripping sound.

"Oh, man!" cried Tim, waving his hand in front of his face.

Harold had passed gas again, an astonishing fart that created another huge cloud of pink and orange gas.

Looking relieved, the woodchuck lunged toward us once more.

We screamed and ran.

"Here!" cried Tim an instant later. "In here!"

It was our own classroom. We scrambled in, then slammed the door behind us.

Tim flicked on the lights.

We heard a muffled thud as the woodchuck flung itself against the door.

Another thud. Another. Then another huge fart.

"I'm not sure how long that door will hold out," said Tim nervously. "Can you use your *sphen-gnut-ksher* on Harold?"

"It would never work on something that large."

The next thud was followed by a cracking sound.

The door was beginning to buckle.

The Veeblax, which was clinging to my neck, shrieked in terror. So did the hamsters.

THUD! CRACK!

"Wait a minute!" cried Tim. "I just realized! I've got something that might help us. Now, if I can just find it . . ."

"What are you talking about?" I cried.

He was busy patting his pockets. "Where is it?" he muttered. "Where is it? Dang. I can't believe I didn't bring it with me." Then his eyes lit up. "Wait a minute! I don't think I even took it home!"

"What are you talking about?" I asked again.

THUD!

That was it. The door splintered and bulged

in. Harold's furry face was pressing against the splinters.

Tim ran to his desk and began rummaging in it. "Where is it?" he muttered desperately. "Where is it?"

"Where is *what?*" I shouted in exasperation.

Harold had nearly bulged his way through the door. He was whistling frantically, a shrill sound that made it nearly impossible to think. His eyes were red and fiery. The Veeblax, still clinging to my shoulder, was whimpering now rather than shrieking.

Tim grabbed the legs of his desk and tipped it up, spilling its contents onto the floor.

"Aha!" he cried, diving for a purple object that looked oddly familiar. He scurried across the room to join me.

Harold was caught in the doorway, but he was pulling himself forward with his claws, which were so powerful they were actually digging into the floor. He stopped to fart again, and a horrible orange and pink cloud billowed up behind him.

Tim popped open the device he had retrieved from his desk.

"Where did you get that?" I asked in astonishment.

"Your Fatherly One gave it to me, so I could contact him if I had any information about where you were." He pressed two buttons. The tiny screen lit up. "This is Tim, calling Meenom. Tim Tompkins, calling Meenom. Emergency. *Emergency!*"

He had to shout to be heard above the cacophony in the classroom—Harold's piercing whistle, the rending sound of the wood as he pushed his way through it, the terrified shrieks of the Veeblax.

Just as the comm-device was connecting, we heard a sound in the hallway.

"Speektam brechlij keebo!" cried an unfamiliar voice.

Harold made it all the way into the room. He reared up on his hind legs, just as he had when Larrabe held up the carrot for him, only it was a lot less cute now that he was nearly eight feet tall. He farted again, and the horrid pink and orange cloud of his gas drifted around our knees. His shadow loomed over us. He swayed back and forth, and now his whistles held a

tragic note that seemed filled with desperate longing.

A noise at the doorway distracted Harold. He swung to see what it was. On the far side of his huge, furry bulk I saw two off-worlders wearing dark brown uniforms. The Interplanetary Animal Control Team! But they had come expecting to retrieve a relatively harmless little Veeblax. When the giant woodchuck lurched toward them with an ear-piercing shriek, they cried out in terror and fled.

One of them dropped its ray gun.

"Tim!" I cried. "That ray gun has a powerful tranquilizer beam. If we can distract Harold long enough for one of us to get it, we might be able to immobilize the monster."

"All right," he replied. "Who gets the wood-chuck, and who gets the gun?"

"It seems to have been after me all the time," I said nervously. "So I guess I'm the one who should distract it."

I began to edge away from Tim.

The giant woodchuck kept its glittering red eyes fixed on me. It whistled again, the sound shrill and horrible, but somehow pathetic.

And then, finally, I figured it all out.

Reaching into my coat pocket, I pulled out the pouch of Veeblax chow and flung it across the room.

With a squeal, Harold lurched after it, scattering desks and chairs in all directions.

Tim dived across the room and grabbed the ray gun. "How do you use this dang thing?" he cried.

"Bring it here!" I shouted. "Quick!"

Harold had snatched up the package of Veeblax chow, pathetically tiny in his enormous paws, and was tearing at it with his huge front teeth.

Tim handed me the ray gun. I adjusted the dial and pulled the trigger.

A purple beam shot out, striking Harold squarely in the rump. He emitted one last, horrible fart, then swayed to the side, caught himself, swayed again, and toppled to the floor with a muffled *whump!*

CHAPTER
20
[LINNSY]

The Truth at Last

Once I had the truth from Misty, it took me almost an hour to figure out how to get a message to the embassy. Finally I called Ms. Weintraub, who gave me the number for McNally's cell phone.

Less than ten minutes after I had told him what was going on, the limousine squealed to a stop in front of Misty's house.

While Misty left a note for her parents, I called my mother to tell her I would be at the embassy,

Then the two of us piled into the car.

"Man," said Misty as we settled into the seat

beside McNally, "what a car. You've even got a chauffeur! I feel like a movie star."

I saw Ralph-the-Driver glance into the mirror. But he didn't say anything. According to Tim and Pleskit, he never does. I didn't say anything, either, even though Misty's comment really annoyed me. It was as if she felt she was getting a reward, when what she deserved was . . . well, I don't know what she deserved, but it wasn't a reward. But I was afraid if I said anything, she would get in one of her moods and refuse to cooperate.

So I kept my mouth shut.

Misty continued to be wide-eyed and astonished as we drove up to Thorncraft Park, where the embassy hangs from its great hook. We entered the tunnel that leads to the underground entrance, then, after getting out of the limo, took the "pipe" that carries visitors up the curve of the hook to the main hallway.

Ms. Buttsman was there to meet us. "The ambassador is tied up with an interplanetary call," she said, her voice dripping ice. "After that, he has to speak to the president. He'll be with you as soon as he can. Until then, you can wait here."

She showed us to a couple of purple seats. They were more comfortable than they looked.

We waited.

And waited.

And waited.

After a while Shhh-foop came in with a tray of snacks. The sight of a six-foot-tall orange alien with tentacles growing out of her head nearly sent Misty into hysterics, and she was not able to sample the snacks. I tried a couple. One was way too salty. The other was sweet, and I think I might have been able to learn to like it, but the way it wiggled on my tongue was a little too weird for me to want any more right then, especially since I was so keyed up.

Almost three hours dragged by before we were finally escorted into Meenom's office.

He was sitting in his command pod. "Greetings, girls," he said solemnly. "My apologies for making you wait so long, but we are in a state of deep crisis right now." He paused, then said, "I understand you have some information for me."

It wasn't easy to get Misty to repeat her story, and I had just gotten her started when something in the command pod made an alarming sound.

"Wait!" said Meenom sharply. He touched a roller ball.

Misty gasped. Well, so did I. An image of Tim's face had appeared in the air in front of us.

"Tim Tompkins calling Meenom!" it said. "Emergency. *Emergency!*"

We heard some weird noises, and Tim's face disappeared.

Meenom, looking terribly alarmed, shouted for McNally. Misty and I managed to stay attached to the group as we hurried to the limousine.

"Where are we going?" asked McNally.

"Follow the tracking device," said Meenom, passing a round, purple object to Ralph-the-Driver. *"Quickly!"*

I didn't know limos could go that fast.

Misty told Meenom most of her story while we were riding. She was just finishing when the limo pulled up in front of the school.

McNally and Meenom shot out of the car and hurried toward the building. I glanced at Misty. She nodded, and the two of us took off after them.

By the time they reached our classroom, we were right at their heels.

We had to pick our way over the splintered remains of the door to get inside. Once we did, we found the most astonishing sight: Tim and Pleskit, sitting on top of an eight-foot-long woodchuck. The Veeblax was scampering back and forth between them, changing shape as it went, as if it was so excited it couldn't hold one form for long.

"What in the name of Skatwag's Seven Moons has been going on here?" roared Meenom.

Pleskit immediately looked frightened. "You can't take the Veeblax!" he cried, snatching up the little creature and cradling it to his chest.

"I don't intend to," said Meenom, though his voice was still stern. "We have some new information that has altered the situation. But what is this . . . this *thing* that you are sitting on? And where did you get that animal control

device?" he added, gesturing to the ray gun that Pleskit was holding.

"Uh . . . we dropped it, sir," said a voice from behind us.*

Meenom swung around. Standing just outside the doorway were two uniformed aliens. One looked rather like a fish. The other looked astonishingly human, or would have if it hadn't been for her four eyes.

"You *dropped* it?" roared Meenom.

"We were not advised that we would be facing such a large creature," said the fishy-looking alien. "Our assignment was to collect a Veeblax, not a huge, furry monster."

"So you let my childling and his friend immobilize the creature instead?" asked Meenom scornfully.

The fishy-looking alien held up a webbed hand. The other alien folded her hands over her chest and closed three of her four eyes.

Meenom made a noise that could only mean disgust. Turning back to Pleskit, he said, "Do

---

* Actually, what the voice said was *Deetpo izzle skittin perdangi.* Pleskit translated it, and the rest of the conversation that follows, for me afterward.

you have any idea where this creature came from?"

Pleskit bowed his head and said, "I fear its existence is my fault, O Fatherly One. I believe that after it escaped from its cage it began to eat the food I had brought to school for the Veeblax. In fact, I suspect it escaped specifically to get at the food, which it seemed to find most enticing. Alas, the Veeblax chow caused Harold to grow at a bizarre rate."

"We think he got addicted to the stuff," added Tim. "He's been following Pleskit everywhere, trying to get more."

"Only he's naturally a pretty shy kind of creature," added Pleskit. "So he didn't actually come after me until his cravings were out of control. At least, that's our theory."

"The Veeblax chow had one other side effect," said Tim. "It seems to have affected Harold's digestive system. He's been cutting farts o' doom that just about stripped the paint off the wall. I was afraid they were going to kill us all!"

Meenom turned to the aliens standing outside the door. "As you have utterly failed in your assigned mission, why don't you make yourself useful and take this poor creature to be returned to his normal size?"

"They won't hurt him, will they?" cried Pleskit as the alien animal control officers attached what I can only assume were antigravity disks to Harold's bloated body and floated him out of the room.

"They're merely going to detoxify him," said Meenom. "The creature will be fine when they're done—which is more than I can say for you," he added darkly. His face softened a little. "Fortunately—and largely due to your friend Linnsy—the Veeblax has gotten a reprieve."

"It has?" cried Pleskit. The joy in his voice was wonderful to hear.

"What happened?" cried Tim.

"Tell them," said Meenom, turning to Misty.

Sniffing a little, obviously working to keep from breaking out in tears, Misty said, "The reason the Veeblax glommed on to me that day was that I snitched some Veeblax chow and put it in my shirt pocket."

"What did you do that for?" asked Pleskit, looking totally confused.

Misty wiped her arm across her face to take care of her nose, which was starting to run. "I w-w-w-wanted to get the Veeblax to come to me," she snuffled.

"Why didn't you say something before this?" demanded Pleskit.

"I w-w-w-was afraid! And the longer things went on, the m-m-m-more afraid I got. I haven't been able to s-s-s-sleep all week because I w-w-w-was so upset."

I wanted to whack her. After all that everyone had been through because of her little stunt, she wanted us to feel sorry for *her!* But that was just like Misty.

"That's not enough," said Pleskit.

I blinked in surprise. "What do you want?" I asked. "Should I get her to sign a confession in blood?"

"Euuuw," said Pleskit. "That would be disgusting! No, I mean it's not enough to explain the Veeblax's behavior that day. Yes, the Veeblax chow in her pocket would have made it jump for Misty like that. But it certainly wouldn't have made it cling to her so desperately."

At that moment the Veeblax let out a horrible

shriek. It began to shudder and moan, vibrating as if it were in a blender.

Then, to my astonishment and horror, its foot fell off!

"That's it!" cried Pleskit happily. "At last it all makes sense!"

CHAPTER
21
[TIM]

Biology

When the Veeblax's foot fell off, I screamed.

"No, no, it's fine," said Pleskit. "The Veeblax is getting ready to reproduce. *That's* why it acted that way the other day with Misty. When a shapeshifter enters *gorkle,* it is in a needy and unstable situation. I knew the food alone wasn't enough to explain what happened. And just going into *gorkle* wouldn't have done it, either. But the two situations together . . . well, I'm sure that's what happened."

"I believe you are correct, my childling," said Meenom.

"Care to translate for those of us who are not

totally up to speed on the biology of alien pets?" asked Linnsy.

"Certainly," said Pleskit. "Like all Hevi-Hevian shapeshifters, the Veeblax has two modes of reproduction. One is a fairly standard mating practice, much like most higher animals on Earth. But if a Veeblax is taken from its normal surroundings, or deprived of a mating complex, or both, then it may go into *gorkle* instead."

"And just what is *gorkle?*" asked Misty.

"Let me think for a second," said Pleskit, and I could tell he was running through everything he knew about the biology of Earth animals. "Okay," he said after a minute. "When a shapeshifter like the Veeblax goes into *gorkle,* it is getting ready to create a new life unit. This can make its behavior somewhat erratic. The process goes on for several days, and when the new unit is ready to exist on its own, the shapeshifter seals off a piece of itself, then separates that piece from its body."

He bent down and picked up the Veeblax's foot. As he did, I saw that the Veeblax had already reshaped itself, forming a new foot to replace the one that had fallen off. That was when I realized that losing a body part is not the same for a shapeshifter as it is for a normal animal.

Pleskit held up the Veeblax piece that had fallen off. "This is known as an *oog-slama*. It is like a cross between an egg and a cocoon. The new Veeblax will develop inside of this. But rather than breaking out, when the creature is finally ready to enter the world, it will simply absorb this outer skin and begin to change shape. Anyway, it was the delicate chemical condition that occurs just prior to the start of *gorkle* that made the Veeblax latch on to Misty in such an uncharacteristic fashion—though it would not have done so at all had she not been toting the Veeblax chow in her pocket."

"I think that will be sufficient to calm the Trading Council," said Meenom. "Whether it will satisfy the Earth media is another issue. Though that, combined with Misty's confession, should settle things down a bit. However, that still leaves one issue left to resolve— namely what should be done with the Veeblax-to-be?"

Pleskit held up the *oog-slama* and smiled. "I think I have a good idea, but it will require the approval of one additional party."

That additional party turned out to be my mother, though it was the next day before we were able to talk to her about Pleskit's idea.

Her first reaction was not promising. She looked at Pleskit and Meenom in astonishment and said, "Are you serious?"

"We believe Tim has earned the honor," replied Meenom solemnly.

Mom wrinkled up her face. "But . . . but . . ."

"I'll take good care of it, Mom. I promise!"

She was starting to look trapped.

"It doesn't need to be walked," I said quickly.

"And we will gladly provide the food," added Pleskit, "so it will be no additional expense. Also, a Veeblax is relatively odor free."

I was getting ready to do the ultra-beg, though I was a little nervous about demonstrating the technique, which involves flinging myself to the floor and grabbing Mom's feet, in front of Pleskit and Meenom.

Luckily, I didn't have to resort to such desperate measures. Mom sighed. Then she smiled and said, "All right, Tim. I guess it's time you had a pet. But you'd better take good care of it, buster!"

"I will," I said, cradling the *oog-slama* in my hands. "I promise!"

And I plan to.

CHAPTER
22
[PLESKIT]

A Letter Home

FROM: Pleskit Meenom, on the ever-stressful Planet Earth
TO: Maktel Geebrit, on the beloved but far too distant Planet Hevi-Hevi

Dear Maktel:

Well, there you have it—the story of my latest misadventure here on Earth. I certainly hope it is more fun to read these things than it is to live through them.

The Fatherly One and I have had several counseling sessions with *Wakkam* Akkim, who truly is a wisebeing. The Fatherly One understands better now how I feel about him being gone so much. And I understand better why he is gone so much.

Things are not completely solved. But they are getting better. And as *Wakkam* Akkim says, "A journey of a thousand *pigskuri* starts not with the first step, but with figuring out the right direction."

The other good news is that the Fatherly One called and talked to the school superintendent, and Ms. Weintraub is no longer in danger of being transferred.

I think he enjoyed that conversation. After all the tough negotiating he must do every day he said that it was fun to intimidate a self-important minor bureaucrat, though he was a little sorry that he made the man cry.

Oops. Have to take a break here. Barvgis just came to my door with the mail pouch, and I want to see if there are any messages from you.

Well, there was a message, as you probably already knew. And what a message. I can't believe you are finally coming to visit—much less that you will be here in less than an Earthly month!

Oh, Maktel, I will be so glad to see you. I can't wait to show you this strange world and introduce you to my new friends. (Or should that be "show you this new world, and introduce you to my strange friends"? Just kidding! I like my new friends a lot. I am sure you'll all get along!)

We're going to have So Much Fun!

I just hope we don't also have any new catastrophes while you are here.

Travel safely, Maktel. I will be awaiting your arrival.

Fremmix Bleeblom!

Your pal,
Pleskit

About the Author and the Illustrator

BRUCE COVILLE, the author of more than seventy-five books for young readers, was born in Syracuse, New York. He grew up in a rural area north of the city, around the corner from his grandparents' dairy farm, where he often dreamed of traveling to other planets. His favorite writers included Hugh Lofting, Eleanor Cameron, and (a little later) Edgar Rice Burroughs.

In the years before he began making his living as a writer, Bruce worked as a gravedigger, a toymaker, an elementary-school teacher, and a magazine editor (among other things). Now he mostly writes, but also spends a fair amount of time traveling to speak at schools and conferences. He also produces and directs unabridged recordings of fantasy novels for children.

Bruce and his wife, Katherine, live in an old brick house in Syracuse, which they share with a number of strange animals and whichever of their three children happens to be home at the moment.

Bruce's best-known books include *My Teacher Is an Alien, Goblins in the Castle,* and *The Skull of Truth.*

TONY SANSEVERO received his art education from Boston's Massachusetts College of Art. He has illustrated several picture books and teen novels, and is an award-winning fine artist as well. He lives in Syracuse, New York, with a menagerie of weird animals and his collection of sci-fi toys.

On the following pages you will find
the thrilling conclusion of
"Disaster on Geembol Seven"
—Pleskit's story of what happened
on the last planet where he lived before
coming to Earth.

DISASTER ON GEEMBOL SEVEN

Part Six:
"Desperate Gamble"

FROM: Pleskit Meenom, on Planet Earth
TO: Maktel Geebrit, on Planet Hevi-Hevi

Dear Maktel:

The time has come to finish the story of what happened on Geembol Seven. As you probably remember, shortly after I arrived on the planet, I was abducted by Balteeri, one of those half-biological, half-mechanical "constructs" most of the galaxy thought had vanished after the Delfiner War. He and a six-eyed boy named Derrvan claimed to need my help.

They took me deep into the planet, to a secret city Derrvan's father had created for the constructs who survived the war. Now the city was doomed, for an earthquake was coming that would topple the place around them. But the constructs could not leave, because a secret branch of the Geembolian government existed specifically to keep them trapped inside the planet, as part of a shameful agreement made after the war.

I learned all this from a *serha* named Dombalt.

As if to prove her story, a small earthquake struck just after she finished telling it. That was when I knew I had to help, no matter what it cost me.

"One thing is not yet clear to me," I said, still trembling from the experience of the earthquake. "If you are blockaded in here, how did Balteeri get out?"

"We have routes by which a single construct, or even a handful, can escape the caverns," said Balteeri. "But there are over forty-thousand of us here. There is no way we could hide it if we all tried to leave at once. The construct hunters would consider it an invasion and attack us in force. Even if they didn't wipe us out completely, there would be thousands of deaths on both sides."

Derrvan spoke for the first time in quite a while. "Balteeri came to get me because I was the only organic they felt certain they could count on to try to help. But what can I do? I have no connections to those in power. But you do, Pleskit. You must speak for us. You can get the story heard, which is the only thing that can save us."

I knew that he was right. Yet the idea of so many beings depending on me was far more terrifying than any mere earthquake.

"We'll have to get back to the surface," I said, trying not to let my fear sound in my voice.

"Unfortunately, we can't go back the way we came," said Balteeri. "Not only have the construct hunters destroyed that exit, but they'll be keeping an extra watch on it now, in case we try to open it again. That means I will have to leave you a fair distance from your home, since I dare not get too close to the city." He must have seen my look of surprise, because he added, "It is not personal fear that makes me say that, Pleskit. It's just that if I am seen, it will alert the construct hunters and may make it impossible for you to get your message out. You must understand that they are ruthless, will stop at nothing. You will have to be on your guard at all times."

"Stop, Balteeri," said *Serha* Dombalt. "You'll terrify the boy!"

"He has to know what he is getting into," said Balteeri grimly.

"It's all right," I said. "All I need to do is contact the Fatherly One, and I will be retrieved very quickly."

"I will not even be able to take you directly to a populated spot," said Balteeri. "You will have to walk some distance."

"I can cope with that."

Balteeri nodded. "Good. We should leave immediately."

"You'll need this," said *Serha* Dombalt. She pulled a shiny black card from her robe and held it out to me. I recognized it as an old-fashioned image-holder. "This contains pictures of our city, interviews with some of our people, information about the coming earthquake. It will help you prove what you have to say to the people of Geembol."

I took the card and tucked it into one of my inner pockets. It was a tiny thing on which to hang the lives of forty thousand beings.

"I'll come with you," said Derrvan.

"That's a bad idea," said Balteeri. "If you are caught by the construct hunters and they realize who you are, it will go especially hard with you. They will see you as a mortal enemy."

"I have to speak for my father's work," said Derrvan firmly.

I looked at him in surprise. This was a much different boy than the weeping one who had lured me to the docks.

"I think he needs to go," said *Serha* Dombalt softly. "Pleskit is the key to getting someone in power to listen, but Derrvan can confirm the story—especially if anyone has the brains to consult some history. After all, he is his father's son."

Balteeri hesitated, then said, "All right, let's go." He turned to *Serha* Dombalt. Placing his face gently against hers, he whispered, "I'll come back as soon as I can. I want to be here with you, no matter what happens."

She put her hand—the metallic one, with its six odd fingers—against his cheek. "I'll be waiting," she replied, her voice husky.

I turned away, startled. It was odd to think of constructs having such tender feelings. I examined my startlement and realized it had nothing to do with the constructs, and everything to do with the lies I had been taught about the Delfiner War.

We returned to the ship that Balteeri had piloted so skillfully to carry us down to the secret city.

Of our journey back to the surface there is little to say, other than that it was terrifying. Though we were not pursued, Balteeri flew through such narrow passages, and at such an amazing speed, that I thought my death would come at any second. Finally he brought the vessel to rest in a small cavern. "All right," he said, "from here on we walk."

Making one of his mechanical parts glow, he led us into a series of winding passages.

We didn't talk much along the way, partly because it was tiring work, at least for me, and partly because often we were walking single file, squeezing through narrow stone corridors. But Balteeri did say one thing that I could not get out of my mind.

"*Serha* Dombalt has more faith in the rulers of this planet than I do. I think our only hope lies with the people. They would demand action if they knew the truth."

We emerged from a small cave onto the side of a steep hill overlooking the sea. The sun was just rising over the green water. An enormous *gabill-fish* broke the surface, its silver-blue body flashing in the morning light. The last and smallest of the twelve moons still lingered in the sky, but the Night of the Moondance was over. I was stumbling from exhaustion, which made sense, as I had gone the entire night with no sleep.

"Where are we?" I asked, trying to stifle a *snarz-bizip*.

"A half day's walk north of the city," said Balteeri. "Do you think you'll be able to make it back all right?"

161

He looked nervous, and I realized that once he left us, he would have no way to force me to keep my promise. Nor, I realized, could he protect us. He wouldn't even know if Derrvan and I made it to the city to deliver our message.

"We'll be all right," I said, trying to sound braver than I felt. "I'll do all I can. I promise."

Balteeri nodded. Then he clasped my shoulders with three of his hands and said, "The lives of forty thousand beings are in your care." He stared at me for a moment, his organic eye and his mechanical one both seeming to pierce right through me. Then he turned and disappeared back into the cave.

Derrvan and I started down the steep hillside. I longed to rest but didn't dare. The final earthquake might not come for days, or even a full *grinnug*. But it might as easily come in the next hour, and I was terrified by the idea that taking time to rest could mean the difference between life and death for an entire city.

Yet we could not run the whole distance. Our bodies simply would not do it. Fortunately, I did not think that would be necessary. I expected to find a communication post well before we got back. Once I could call in, I knew we would be picked up very quickly.

Even so, we did run part of the way. When we stopped to walk, Derrvan told me about his life, how his mother—he had a direct mother, not a Motherly One—had taught him about his father's work from the time he was old enough to listen.

"It was a strange secret to have," he said. "I did not talk about it with friends."

"Why not?"

He closed four of his six eyes. "Partly because it happened so long ago. My father died hundreds of *grinnugs* before I was born, you know, so the story was almost like a fairy tale to me. But the bigger reason I didn't talk about it was because my friends all think of constructs as monsters. They have no idea of them other than what they have experienced in terror-ramas." He paused, then added, "It has been my dream since I was little to redeem my father's work."

We had come to a road by this time. "Look!" I cried. "A comm-pole! Come on!"

We ran, stumbling and gasping, to the thick green and purple pole. I keyed in my code, got a connection, then keyed in the second code that would put me through to the embassy.

"Barvgis!" I cried when the connection was made and I saw his round face on the pole's viewscreen. "It's me, Pleskit!"

"Pleskit!" he shouted, and it made me feel good to hear the relief in his voice. "Where are you? Your Fatherly One has been frantic with fear!"

I gave him the locator numbers for the pole.

"We'll have someone there soonest," said Barvgis.

Since we needed to stay where we were in order to be picked up, I felt I could finally relax for a little while. Leaning against the commpole, I closed my eyes. The day was warm, the smells of Geembol Seven mostly sweet and pleasant. But I didn't relax, of course. All I could think of was what I had to do, and how many people's lives depended on it.

I don't know how much time had gone by before Derrvan shook my arm and said, "Pleskit, they're here!"

I leaped to my feet, which actually made Derrvan laugh. Three hovercars drifted to the ground in front of us. The tops of the cars lifted.

Each was piloted by a Geembolian Safety Officer. I watched as the driver of the first car climbed out, its stilt-like legs lifting the glistening, transparent cap of its body.

I was disappointed to see that the Fatherly One was not in any of the vehicles.

The Safety Officer seemed to understand the look on my face. "Your Fatherly One was at Safety Central, monitoring our search for you. Our patrol was much closer to this spot than he is, and when we got word where you were, we came directly here. Your parental unit will be waiting for you when we get back."

I was mostly relieved by this information—though I was also nervous about how the Fatherly One was going to react to the story I had to tell.

As things worked out, I was not able to consult with the Fatherly One before matters came to a head. When we reached the city, we found a group of reporters clustered around the Safety Central media platform, all waiting to interview me.

An array of transmission and recording devices was ready and waiting to beam my words around the planet even as I spoke them.

I knew enough about the news media to realize that as the lost child of the off-world ambassador I was a big story, a story that was probably being followed by hundreds of millions of beings who would be eager to hear what had happened to me.

And as I thought of that vast audience, I remembered Balteeri's words in the tunnel: *Our only hope lies with the people. They would demand action if they knew the truth.*

With a thrill of terror and excitement I understood that when I stepped to the microphone, I would be speaking directly to the people.

No one would be expecting me to say anything controversial.

No censor would be on guard, waiting to pull the plug.

I was being handed a chance, a single golden chance, to tell the people themselves of the strange prison that existed inside their world, of the "ancient wrong so foul that the memory of it cries to the stars."

All it would take was some courage, and the willingness to do something that I knew full well would likely destroy the Fatherly One's mission on Geembol Seven.

What I did not take into account—could not take into account, because I had no way of understanding it—was the desperation of the construct hunters, the lengths to which they would go to keep their evil secret.

Derrvan stood to the side, between two of the Safety Officers. We both knew that in the minds of the reporters, I was the story. I would introduce him as soon as possible, but for now, it was all up to me.

I stepped to a speaking device.

"First things first," said the Geembolian whom this group of reporters had selected to be their spokesbeing. "Are you all right?" Her internal organs, clearly visible through the transparent cap of her body, were moving sluggishly, a sign that she was relaxed.

(I have to stop to mention that this experience was utterly unlike it would have been on Earth, where the reporters would all have been shouting at the same time.)

"I'm fine," I said, trying to sound cheerful, to put them at ease.

"Thank the moons for that," said the lead reporter. "Now, what, exactly, happened to you?"

"I was taken on a surprise tour of one of Geembol's less-known scenic areas." I chose my words carefully, for I feared that if I mentioned the constructs too quickly I might be cut off—or, perhaps even worse, that people would stop listening before I could say what was truly important. "It was remarkable, a hidden wonder of your planet that is in danger of being destroyed."

"How can that be?" asked the reporter. She sounded offended, and I noticed her organs were moving a bit faster now. "We guard our world most carefully."

"This place is unknown to all save a few of your leaders," I said. "And those few have worked tirelessly to keep it secret from you."

An uneasy murmur rippled through the crowd of reporters. This was not a polite thing to say, and politeness is highly valued on Geembol Seven. I suspect some even thought I had gone crazy. Most, however, wanted to know what I was talking about.

I smiled. Arousing their curiosity had been my main goal.

It was a trick I had learned from the Fatherly One.

"I was taken to visit a city hidden deep beneath the surface of your planet. I have pictures of it." I pulled out the card *Serha* Dombalt had given me.

"Who lives in this city?" asked the lead reporter, clearly startled by my claim.

"It is the home of—"

My words were cut off by Derrvan, who hurtled in from the side of the platform and flung himself against me, knocking me away from the microphone.

At the same moment an orange ray shot down from a nearby rooftop. It struck my side, slicing a wound that felt like fire. Had Derrvan not pushed me out of the way, it would have struck me full in the chest.

Alas, that was exactly what happened to him. I heard his scream, and the sizzle of his flesh even as I hit the platform.

Chaos erupted. The reporters were screaming and shouting. The Safety Officers, shaking their fringes in fury, closed protectively around us. Before they could block me in, I crawled to the edge of the platform. Thrusting *Serha* Dombalt's image holder ahead of me, I passed it to the lead reporter.

"Show this to the world," I pleaded. "To the people. Forty thousand lives depend on it."

Clutching my wounded side, I crawled back to where Derrvan had fallen, pushing my way through the legs of the Safety Officers who were standing, ray guns ready, trying to spot the assassin.

At the center of the platform were other officers who had retracted their legs and settled the caps of their bodies close to the floor. They were clustered around Derrvan, their tentacles twitching in horror as they made a mournful keening sound.

No one was touching him.

He held out a hand to me. Ignoring the blazing pain in my side, I crawled to him, took his hand in mine.

"It was a construct hunter," he whispered,

squeezing my fingers. "I saw him on the roof across the street, just before he fired." He coughed, and it was a horrible noise. Two of his eyes had closed. Another had filmed over and gone dim.

"I slipped the image holder to the lead reporter," I said. "We got the word out, Derrvan. The people will know the truth."

"I know," he said.

Then he closed the rest of his eyes.

His hand went limp.

I raised my face to the sky and added my voice to the wail of the Geembolians.

The lead reporter had done her job well. Within an hour *Serha* Dombalt's image holder was fed into the news networks. It wasn't long before the entire planet knew not only the story of Construct City, but the way the construct hunters tried to assassinate me to prevent the truth from coming out.

The government of Geembol Seven fell the next day.

The fury and disgust of the people was incredible. Oddly enough, one of the things they were most angry about was that the construct hunters had suspected where I was and had not spoken out during the time that my being missing was the top story on the planet.

That was why a construct hunter had been waiting to assassinate me, of course: The hunters had linked my abduction with the chase that Balteeri had led them on. They didn't know exactly what was happening when I came back, but they were pretty sure where I had been, and were afraid of what I might say.

The Safety Officers had not been guarding against any such thing because they had no reason to expect it. After all, they didn't even know the construct hunters existed.

Even though the fall of the government was not really my fault, the Trading Federation canceled the Fatherly One's charter and pulled us from the planet. It is not considered appropriate for Traders to get involved in local politics, much less cause a revolution. And, as I was told several times, I had broken a major rule by making an end run around "proper channels" in order to take the story straight to the people.

*   *   *

Well, there you have it, Maktel. Now you can understand the reason I have been so reluctant to talk about this. It brings up very painful memories.

Though the Fatherly One was greatly disturbed by what happened, he has also told me I did the right thing.

He even said I was a hero.

That is not true, of course. All I did was pass along a story.

The real hero was Derrvan.

I barely knew him, Maktel. Yet I cannot think of him without my *clinkus* tightening with pain. He saved my life, and in doing so lost his own.

But we also saved the constructs.

Forty thousand souls brought back from the brink of death.

That's something, don't you think?

Worth getting thrown off a planet for, if you ask me.

Your pal,
Pleskit

A Glossary of Alien Terms

Following are definitions for the alien words and phrases appearing for the first time in this book. Definitions of extraterrestrial words used in earlier volumes of *I Was a Sixth Grade Alien* can be found in the book where they were first used.

For most words we are only giving the spelling. In actual usage many would, of course, be accompanied by smells and/or body sounds.

The number after a definition indicates the chapter where the word first appears.

A complete glossary of alien words from *all* the *I Was a Sixth Grade Alien* books can be found at www.brucecoville.com.

deefrim: slang term, shortened from *deefrim ub <large belch> okpit* meaning, literally, "cough up an internal organ." Used to describe someone showing great shock, fear, or surprise. (12)

gerdin poozlit: To massage one's forehead with one's knuckles. This is a comfort activity for newly hatched Hevi-Hevians, not unlike thumb-sucking for Earthling infants. It is considered very inappropriate for anyone who has been out of the shell for more than a *grinnug.* (7)

gorkle: A state of solo reproductive readiness experienced by all seven species in Hevi-Hevi's shapeshifting genus when they are forced to live in long-term isolation from others of their kind. Under the right circumstances a shapeshifter in *gorkle* undergoes a splitting process not unlike that of an amoeba. However, the work at the cellular level is much more sophisticated, and the body division is not equal, so that there is a definite parent-child relationship. (21)

kalyap: A vicious predator that lurks at the edge of the swampfields of Hevi-Hevi. *Kalyappi* (plural) are especially feared because of their tenacious grasp, which does not relax even when the creatures are killed.

kirgiltum: The internal organ where food is stored prior to digestion, often referred to by children as *oodli skimbat* ("my little pantry"); connected by the *clinkus* to the respiratory system. (7)

oog-slama: (plural: *oogle-slamini*) The developmental organ expelled by a shapeshifter that has run a complete cycle of *gorkle.* A cross between an egg and a cocoon, *oogle-slamini* are considered special delicacies by the gourmets of Hevi-Hevi, though there has been a recent popular movement to discourage people from eating them. (21)

plissinga: A student who has willingly bound him, her, or itself to a teacher of spiritual matters. One cannot become a *plissinga* until one has reached *vershniffle.* (3)

snarz-bizip: a sudden, loud snort through the nose, made when a Hevi-Hevian is very tired, or drifting off to sleep; often accompanied by a spray of sparks from the *sphen-gnut-ksher*. (serial episode)

Speektam brechlij keebo: Not Hevi-Hevian, and difficult to translate exactly. The general sense is "What the heck is that thing?" (19)

vershniffle: Literally, "The second awakening." Refers to the time when a Hevi-Hevian is ready to receive more intense spiritual training. (Hevi-Hevians believe that children should glory in the physical world, and fear that spiritual training given too early may stifle the full awakening of the wonder and awe they will experience when undergoing training in the Deeper Mysteries.) (3)

wakkam: (plural: *wakkamami*) A teacher or guru adept in spiritual training. The Trading Federation believes it is important for anyone involved in business to maintain a balance between work and spirit, and no being is allowed to become a full Trader until a

wakkam has accepted his, her, or its appli-
cation to be a *plissinga*. (This does not represent a forced belief system, by the way, as
the *wakkamami* registered with the Trade
Federation represent over 24,000 different
sects, faiths, and belief systems. Morever, a
Trader may have many *wakkamami* in a
lifetime) (3)

BRUCE COVILLE'S

The fascinating and hilarious adventures of
the world's first purple sixth grader!

I WAS A SIXTH GRADE ALIEN

THE ATTACK OF THE TWO-INCH TEACHER

I LOST MY GRANDFATHER'S BRAIN

PEANUT BUTTER LOVER BOY

ZOMBIES OF THE SCIENCE FAIR

DON'T FRY MY VEEBLAX!

TOO MANY ALIENS
(coming in July 2000)

by Bruce Coville

A MINSTREL® BOOK

Published by Pocket Books

2304-01

Bruce Coville's
Magic Shop Books

THE MONSTER'S RING

Russell is shocked when he finds out what can happen after three twists of the monster's ring.

JEREMY THATCHER, DRAGON HATCHER

She was just a little dragon until she grew, and grew, and grew.

JENNIFER MURDLEY'S TOAD

What do you do when your talking toad has an attitude?

THE SKULL OF TRUTH

It's talking, and it won't shut up!

 A MINSTREL® BOOK

Published by Pocket Books

2054

William knows that Toad-in-a-Cage Castle has its share of hidden mysteries. But in the midnight hours, he has to wonder what could possibly be making those strange moans echoing through the castle's halls.

Then one night he finds out . . . .

"A shivery treat for readers, who will identify with the stalwart William as he ferrets out the castle's scary secrets and rights a long-existing wrong."— ALA Booklist

Goblins
in the
Castle

By Bruce Coville

Available from Minstrel® Books
Published by Pocket Books